DEATH MOUNTAIN

Sherry Shahan

PEACHTREE
ATLANTA

ö

A Freestone Publication

Published by
PEACHTREE PUBLISHERS
1700 Chattahoochee Avenue
Atlanta, Georgia 30318-2112

www.peachtree-online.com

Cover design by Loraine M. Joyner
Book design by Melanie McMahon Ives

Manufactured in United States of America

10 9 8 7 6 5 4 3 2 1
First Edition

Library of Congress Cataloging-in-Publication Data

Shahan, Sherry.
  Death mountain / by Sherry Shahan.-- 1st ed.
     p. cm.
   Summary: While traveling to visit the mother she has not heard from in almost a year, Erin and another teenage girl become lost in the rugged Sierra Nevada mountains and must struggle for six days to survive.
   ISBN 1-56145-353-6
  [1. Survival--Fiction. 2. Sierra Nevada (Calif. and Nev.)--Fiction. 3. Mothers--Fiction. 4. Grandmothers--Fiction.] I. Title.
   PZ7.S52784Dea 2005
   [Fic]--dc22
                                        2005010820

*Especially for my family and friends on the Mt. Whitney
Expedition, 2004: Kristina Beal O'Connor,
Kyle Beal Wommack, Jon Wommack,
Christine Peterson, Jan Bugge, and Holly Stedman*

—S. S.

CHAPTER ONE

Do not go where the path may lead,
go instead where there is no path and leave a trail.
—RALPH WALDO EMERSON

Erin kicked a rusty bottle cap across the two-lane highway in front of the bus station. Another string of RVs rolled by, blocking her view of the rugged Sierra Nevada Mountains. She saw two dirt bikes tied above one of the bumpers. If she had a bike right now, she wouldn't have to break her promise to her grandma about hitchhiking. If her bus ticket hadn't been stolen off her backpack, she'd be two hours down the road by now.

"If wishes were horses," Gram always said, "beggars would ride."

Erin stood on the highway feeling small in the bleak desert. It was my fault, she thought, raking her honey-brown hair into a sloppy braid. I shouldn't have left the ticket in plain sight.

From the moment the plan to visit her mom was proposed, Erin had fought against going. She didn't want to see her no matter where she lived. Not after what she'd done. Leaving like that, without even a good-bye. Just a stupid note saying "I can't take it anymore. I need to find peace...find myself."

"She must have been really lost," Erin muttered, glancing down the highway. "It took her a year just to find a phone."

She rolled her sleeves and scuffed along the gravel shoulder, nearly blown over by the RVs and trucks hurtling by. Across the road, not far from the bus station, a country store leaned in the wind. Heat waves shimmered like ghosts on the asphalt.

"Sorry, Gram," Erin said, sticking out her thumb.

Vehicles blasted by for an hour. Finally a sports car slowed beside her. Sun bounced off the polished hood. As the tinted window rolled down, Erin saw a tanned driver with a capped-tooth grin. "Where're you headed?" he asked.

Erin couldn't see the man's eyes. All she could see in the mirrored lenses of his sunglasses were two pathetically small images of herself. This guy wasn't from the area. His hair was sprayed as stiff as his starched white shirt. Probably from the city.

"Independence," she lied.

"That's south," he said. "You're walking north, toward Lee Vining and Bridgeport."

Erin knew Independence was in the opposite direction of Lee Vining, an hour south of Bishop. She tried to look surprised and turned around, walking back the way she came. The car reversed. She clutched her pack straps, thumbs digging into ribs.

"I wouldn't mind heading north," the man called, "if you were sitting beside me."

What a creep! Erin quickened her pace in a spiral of anger and fear, choking on the dust kicked up by the car's tires. No way could she shake him on foot. Then she spotted a hole in the traffic and darted across the highway. The guy hit his brakes and swerved, tires squealing. Over her shoulder, Erin watched him peel off. She was shivering and sweating at the same time.

If the car had been an old dented truck with a posthole digger in the back and a tailgate crimped with baling wire, Erin wouldn't have made up the story about Independence. She'd learned to rely on country people since moving in with her grandma.

From the other side of the road, the store had looked a hundred years old. Up close it looked even older. The front window was crowded with ads from who knows how long ago: a tattered sign announcing Buzz Buszek's Fly Fishing Tournament, a cardboard placard for Harry's Handyman Tool & Dye, and a poster showing a woman on a tightrope over Niagara Falls. The caption on the poster read, DREAM BIG—DARE TO FAIL.

Inside, the store smelled like sawdust, pickled eggs, and fishing tackle. Local news spilled from a radio behind the counter. "...rescue team organized by the U.S. Forestry department," the announcer said, "to search for a ranger who's been missing in the Sierra Nevada since…"

Erin opened the glass door to the cooler, letting the icy air wash over her. How had she let herself get in such a mess? The bus she was supposed to be on was rambling down the road to Los Angeles, a six-hour trip. From there it was another two-and-a-half hours to Camarillo, a town close to the beach. She'd looked it up on the map right after her mom had called.

* * *

Erin had been sitting on the screened porch that buggy night, sorting leftovers for the worm bin. She wrapped the leftovers for the worms in a newspaper, knowing all traces of food and paper would be gone by morning. Red wigglers would eat anything, but she never fed them meat or cheese. It made the bin stink. Worm droppings produced the best fertilizer for the vegetable garden.

Gram strolled out, her silver gray hair hanging in waves over a loose shirt. "Varnish." She eased herself down on the rickety steps. "That's what these steps need."

Erin smiled.

Gram had been talking about refurbishing the porch ever since Erin and her dad moved in last year. "Your dad's pictures of Cuba are in *The Traveler*," she said, handing Erin the magazine.

4

They sat side by side, flipping through the pages until they saw the words "photographs by Stephen Rowe." Erin stared at the image of a wrinkled woman, a fat cigar in her mouth, and a young boy, his happy brown face smeared with ice cream.

That's what she and Gram had been doing when the phone rang, looking at pictures of old cars and happy brown faces.

Erin followed her grandma into the kitchen.

"Lannie?" Gram whispered. She had a death grip on the receiver, her knuckles as colorless as her cheeks.

Erin stumbled backwards and gripped the counter. "It's Mom?" Trying to get rid of that sick feeling in her stomach, Erin swallowed over and over. She strained to hear the voice on the other side, but only heard Gram's clipped words and half sentences. "Doctor...checked into the hospital...medication."

Erin leaned over the sink.

"Lannie, it's been eleven months..." Gram said, looking shocked and relieved at the same time. "I don't know about these things..."

Erin lost the last remark along with her dinner in the sink. She washed the mess down the drain and rinsed out her mouth.

"Where are you?" Gram asked Erin's mom.

Gram was quiet for a while, listening. Then her face screwed up like a fist. "Wouldn't the doctors let you call?" Her voice was tight. "So we'd at least know you were alive?"

What was going on? Erin couldn't make sense of the conversation.

In the end, her grandmother said, "It isn't up to me. I have to talk to Stephen..."

Gram hung up and placed a call to Erin's dad in Guatemala, where he was on a photo assignment. Erin could tell the hotel operator didn't speak English. Gram struggled to make him understand. "Señor Rowe! Stephen!" Then, she said, "Lannie called.... She sounds fine.... She wants Erin to come for a visit..."

Silence filled the kitchen, like a held breath. Gram listened, rubbing the deep crease between her eyes. Then she hung up and sighed.

"Your father thinks you should go," Gram said.

Erin flared like a struck match. "Why should I?"

Gram moved to the kitchen counter and stood next to Erin. "She wants to see you, little bird."

"Yeah? What about all the times I asked to see her?"

"This is different," Gram said, firm as a cast-iron skillet.

"How?"

"She's your mother."

"Yeah." Erin felt cold inside. "She hatched me."

"You have to go." Gram looked pained. She fiddled at the stove, making herself tea. She left the bag in the cup, as if she needed the extra strength. "Life isn't always fair."

Erin had no doubt about that.

"You have to go," Gram repeated. "So you'll know."

"Know what?"

Gram blew a ripple across her tea. "I promised…"

Erin stared at her grandma's unsettled eyes. Finally Gram shifted uncomfortably. She walked away, her sheepskin slippers silent on the worn pine floor.

Later that night Erin lay awake in bed. She fidgeted restlessly on her side, then on her stomach. She had gotten used to Gram saying things without talking. But that didn't mean she always understood what Gram meant.

Know what? she wondered, trying to fall asleep. What kind of sickness makes a mother leave her family for a year?

Maybe not knowing would be better.

CHAPTER TWO

If nothing ever changed, there'd be no butterflies.
—UNKNOWN

A few days later, Gram knocked on Erin's door. She let herself in when Erin didn't answer and began pulling jeans and T-shirts from the closet. Erin peered over a book of poetry, watching her clothes going into a large-frame backpack. Her room was hot and stuffy. Anger filled her up, making it hard to breathe. Any second she'd either suffocate or explode.

"I'll spend the whole time in my room," she threatened Gram, not trying to hide the defiance in her voice. "Reading and working on my songs."

Gram ignored the remark.

After her grandmother left the room, Erin dumped most of the clothes, replacing them with dog-eared paperbacks. She fell back on her bed and kicked off her sandals, pressing her eyes closed when one shoe banged against the wall.

"No one can make me talk to her," she shouted down the hall.

"It never hurts to listen," Gram shouted back, louder.

Erin thought about the phone call from her mom. She'd probably made up all that stuff about hospitals and doctors. What a lame excuse. Right then and there Erin stopped thinking of her mother as Mom. She didn't deserve to be called Mom, either. Erin settled on her name, Lannie.

Early the next morning Gram and Erin picked at a breakfast of fruit and homemade granola before driving down Highway 395 south to Bishop. A gritty wind blew sand at the pickup truck during the entire two-hour trip. Iron-gray clouds gathered over the distant mountains ringing the desert.

At the bus station, they hugged in the parking lot, jostled by passengers. Erin felt her grandma's breath on her cheek. She wanted to squeeze her with all her might like she used to when she was a kid.

"Los Angeles," a speaker blared.

"Give your mother a chance," Gram said.

"Why should I?" Erin muttered.

A loose strand of unpinned hair tickled Erin's nose. "You have to, Erin," Gram said simply. "Do it for yourself."

Erin didn't want to think about any of this.

"Take care, little bird," Gram said gently.

Erin tried a smile, already missing the way Gram stroked her hair and talked into it at the same time. "I wish you were going with me," Erin said softly as Gram ambled off to the old truck.

Gram didn't hear her.

She was on her way to Bodie to meet friends.

Every year they helped rangers pick up trash—bottles and cans left behind by careless visitors. The volunteers slept in the beds of their trucks and cooked on single-burner stoves along the dirt road leading to the historic ghost town.

Erin loved the beaded Indian clip holding back her grandma's unruly hair and the swing of her tie-dyed skirt. She loved the heavy silver rings with chunky gemstones they'd found in dry creek beds and polished in a rock tumbler. She tried to remember how Lannie dressed. But all she envisioned was her mother's shriveled white skin after soaking in the bathtub all night.

Erin shouldered her backpack, climbed the bus steps, and trudged down the aisle. She dropped into a seat and wiped a circle in the dirty window, watching Gram pull out of the parking lot. Baling wire held up the battered tailgate.

The bus seemed kind of exciting at first—all the people and families. For a few minutes Erin wondered about their lives and where they were headed. But slowly their faces, gray as the seats, blurred into a dull sameness: their expressions said they'd rather be staying home. At least that's how it seemed to Erin.

The engine idled as the last few passengers boarded and stowed their belongings. A cute little dark-haired girl skipped down the aisle, a puppy smuggled under her coat. The bus driver didn't notice.

A pudgy man with whiskers slid in next to Erin, crowding her with his duffel. One whiff said he hadn't bathed in days. Thankfully, the bus driver fired up the air conditioner. Then he rattled off safety instructions. "Everyone must stay in his or her seat while the bus is in motion…"

During the ride from Bishop to Big Pine, the driver pointed at the White Mountains to the east. "…home of the bristlecone pine," he said, "the oldest living tree on earth."

Erin leaned against the window, still clutching her ticket. She hoped the man beside her would get off at the next stop.

"These ancient trees have survived more than forty centuries," the driver droned on. He pointed toward the craggy peaks to the west. "The early Spaniards named these mountains the Sierra Nevada, which means 'snowy mountain range'."

After the geography lesson, the bus rambled into a tiny station. The doors swished open and the engine and air conditioner died. "Big Pine," the driver announced. "Five-minute stop."

The man next to her pulled a can of sardines and a box of crackers from his duffel. "Hungry?" he asked Erin.

The stink of fish mixed with his smelly sweat. "No, thanks," she said and tried to raise her window. She struck the stubborn latch with her palm, choking on the fishy smells. The latch refused to budge.

"Excuse me." Erin climbed over the man. She grabbed her backpack from the rack by the driver and stumbled down the steps into the parking lot. Then she pushed through the crowd in the station, looking for the ladies' room.

Inside the bathroom, she splashed cold water on her face. She dropped her pack outside a stall, setting her ticket on top. She wasn't surprised to find the ticket gone when she came out. She was mad at herself just the same. She might as well have attached a note: Steal me.

Maybe I wanted to lose the ticket, she thought. That way I won't have to see Lannie.

Erin stood alone in the bathroom. No matter how hard she tried she couldn't shake Gram's words, "You have to go—so you'll know."

She went to the ticket counter and explained what had happened.

"Sorry, kid," the woman said. "Your bus just pulled out. Didn't you hear the announcement?"

"No." Had she heard anything while she was in the restroom? Maybe. Maybe not. She hadn't really been paying attention. "I don't want to go to Los Angeles," Erin said. "I want to go home—to Lee Vining."

"Nothing on the schedule until tomorrow morning."

Erin grabbed her pack. "I could walk home by then," she muttered.

Lannie was supposed to meet the bus in Camarillo at 8:00 P.M.

Something inside Erin said, Good, I hope she worries. Something else said, This sucks.

That's when she decided to hitchhike back home.

* * *

The clerk in the country store tapped Erin on the shoulder. "You're gonna let all the cold air out of that cooler."

Erin closed the door, trying to shut out the memory of the guy in the sports car. She picked up a bottle of water, then put it down. Mountain spring water cost more than a soda. Erin snatched a sad-looking apple and two shriveled oranges, and dug a crumpled bill from her pocket. "These aren't worth more than a quarter," she told the clerk.

The clerk shrugged.

"Bet that fruit weighs a pound," someone else said.

Erin turned to see a girl who looked a year or two older than herself, fourteen or fifteen. She had short hair, dyed platinum with purple streaks. "This donut only weighs eight ounces," the girl said. She wore too much sale bin makeup, Erin noticed. "You can eat two donuts and not gain any more weight than eating an apple—if you do the addition right."

Erin wasn't sure if the girl was kidding. "I'd like to meet your math teacher," she said.

Erin went outside and found a bench in the shade. She straddled her pack, in no hurry to return to the highway. It'd be a long walk to Lee Vining. She cut away the brown spots on her apple with her pocketknife. Then she cleaned the blade and returned the knife to the quick-release key ring on her pack.

The girl came out and sat beside her. "Hey, I know you don't know me, but is everything okay? You seem a little...I don't know...upset."

Erin glanced at her.

"My name's Mae. With an *e*, not a *y*."

Erin sighed, "I'm Erin."

"We could give you a ride to Lone Pine," Mae said.

Erin looked around the empty dirt lot. "We?"

"My brother's getting gas," Mae said.

A VW with more than its share of dents pulled up, a plastic sunflower twisted around the antenna. If Erin went with them she'd be further away from Lee Vining, she knew. Lone Pine was in the opposite direction. So what? Gram wasn't home. And why rush back? When Lannie discovered Erin wasn't on the bus she'd probably call Gram's house, and Erin didn't want to talk to her mother. Her dad would be gone at least another week.

Once Erin had asked Gram, "Why can't Dad take pictures closer to home?" Gram had looked pained from head to foot. "It won't be like this forever, Erin."

Erin wasn't sure what she had meant. The last eleven months seemed like forever.

Mae got up from the bench. "Meet Levi," she said, introducing her brother. "And this is Erin. She's hitching a ride with us."

"Hi." Erin tried a smile. "And thanks."

Levi just shrugged.

Mae held the front seat forward while Erin shoved her pack in back and climbed in. She squinted through the bug-splattered window. All the towns on this stretch of highway looked the same. Shops disguised as trading posts selling souvenirs. Sporting goods stores with deer heads mounted above the doors. Restaurants named after mountains: Mt. Whitney Chuck Wagon, Big Baldy Cafe, Snowy Mountain Grille.

Erin caught Levi's annoyed expression in the rearview mirror. His ball cap said MidCoast Tractors. It was square-shaped, the bill too flat. She wanted to bend it for him.

Mae turned on the radio. "No reason to cry," the newscaster said. "Today will be dry." She switched the station to country-western music.

"See the lake we marked? Chicken Springs," Mae said, passing a map over her shoulder. "We're going to hike up and go for a swim. Wanna come?"

A swim sounded good. "Sure."

"One girl is enough," Levi said, an eye on the speedometer. He downshifted through Independence.

Mae slugged him. "Hiking is so hard. Right foot. Left foot."

Levi drummed the steering wheel. "I'm not a baby-sitter," he said with a smirk. Not a dimple anywhere.

"Pull over, please," Erin said, grabbing her pack. She'd rather walk than put up with his attitude.

The VW crept to a stop and she climbed out. "Thanks for the ride."

CHAPTER THREE

*I only went out for a walk and finally concluded
to stay out till sundown, for going out, I found,
was really going in.*

—JOHN MUIR

Erin sat on her pack on the edge of the highway where bone-white tumbleweeds were snagged in a barbed wire fence. A lizard did push-ups on a rock, then scurried for shade. She sucked juice from her orange, shoving peels in her pocket.

The VW whizzed by.

Brake lights flashed.

It backed up.

Mae and Levi again. Now what? she thought.

"We call him Zit," Mae said, opening the door. "Cuz he grows on you."

Erin breathed in so deeply the hot air singed her throat. "Levi or the car?"

"The car." Mae laughed. "Come on, go with us. It'll be fun."

Erin stared at the endless road and its string of RVs and trucks with camper shells, all driven by strangers.

"You can't sit here all day," Mae said.

"Your brain will fry," Levi put in.

Erin drizzled water on her sweaty head. "Too late."

She picked up her pack and climbed back into Zit, feeling like she didn't have any choice. The VW veered off Highway 395. It nearly stalled when the road dipped to a dry creek bed. A sign said, WARN-ING: FLASH FLOOD.

Erin studied the map over Mae's shoulder. It looked like at least an hour drive over switchbacks that zigzagged up the steep granite wall to Horseshoe Meadow Campgrounds, the nearest point to the trailhead leading to Chicken Springs Lake. Her grandma had taught her to read topographic maps on their backpacking trips in the mountains.

The Sierra Nevada was four hundred miles long and eighty miles wide in places, she knew. Structures like bridges and railways were shown in black. Water was blue. Forests, green. The contour lines of mountains and valleys were brown. Lines close together meant the terrain was steep. Small swirling circles indicated peaks.

On their treks, Erin and Gram had passed through the remote high country on the eastern slopes. Hiking off-trail, they could backpack for days and not see anyone. Sometimes they'd go hours without talking. Then one of them would spot a wildflower and they'd stop to look it up in the Audubon field guide.

They passed a second weathered sign: OLD CREEK STABLES. Dark clouds disappeared over the highest ridges. Probably dumping rain on campers on the other side of the mountain, Erin thought. Weather reports are always wrong.

Levi parked the VW by the bathrooms at Horseshoe Meadows, bare-bone campgrounds with a dozen sites that had rock-ringed fire pits, a few with grills and plain wooden tables. Piped water flowed to the bathroom where a dozen bear-proof garbage cans were lined up. A sign by the bathrooms warned: DON'T BE BEAR CARELESS.

Erin got out of the car and read the small print:

Warning: Bear damage is common in this parking area. The sight or odor of food in your vehicle greatly increases the chance of your car being damaged. It is strongly recommended that all food be removed from your vehicle and stored in the bearproof boxes located in this parking lot.

Mae set her knapsack on the ground. It looked more like a big purse with straps than a pack. As she rummaged around inside it, she asked Erin a bunch of questions about what to take to the lake. "Should I wear sandals or sneakers? Do I need socks? What color lipstick should I take?"

Erin wondered if Mae was really that dumb. "Sneakers and socks," she said.

"Don't forget your tiara!" Levi hollered and ducked into the bathroom.

"Is your brother always such a jerk?" Erin asked.

"He tried out for the wrestling team a few days ago—didn't make it."

"So?"

"Our dad's the coach," Mae said. "He's not too happy with Levi right now."

Erin dug through her large-frame backpack, dumping her books on Zit's seat. She hadn't been much of a reader before moving in with Gram. Then she'd discovered books were a safe place to lose yourself. Sitting by the campfire, Gram sometimes read aloud essays by John Muir or Mark Twain. "Both men left their boot marks on this part of California," Gram had said.

Erin shoved nylon bike pants and a sack lunch into her pack, then attached her pocketknife to the outside.

"Don't forget a swimsuit," Mae said.

Erin tied a fleece-lined sweatshirt around her waist. "I don't have one."

She hadn't packed a swimsuit because she hadn't planned on going to the beach with Lannie. She didn't want to go anywhere with her.

Erin headed to the faucet to fill her water bottle, noticing there was only one other group at the campground. Kids in T-shirts with Discovery Bound logos crowded around a picnic table piled with food and gear. Extra hiking boots were tied to the outside of bulging backpacks. So were rain slickers and rolled sleeping bags.

Erin had heard about Discovery Bound, a wilderness survival school for teens in trouble. What had they done to make their parents send them away for three months? What did I do, she thought, to make Lannie leave?

She dodged the answer by checking her watch: 10:20 A.M. Although the sky was clear she knew they should have rain ponchos. Showers were common in this area in summer, no matter what the weather report said. She made a mental note to ask Mae if they had any garbage bags in the VW. In a pinch, a plastic bag could double as a poncho.

"Hey!" one of the teenagers called to her. "Will you take our picture?"

Erin walked over and took the camera. "Sure." She snapped the picture and handed the camera back.

The leader of the Discovery Bound Group wore an official-looking ball cap slapped over gray hair. It said Search and Rescue. He was standing next to a van with a U.S. Forestry Service emblem, fiddling with a two-way radio.

"Excuse me...um...Mr. Sánchez," said Erin, noting the nametag on his shirt. "Are you guys looking for the lost ranger? I heard about him on the news."

Mae came up beside her. "Rangers get lost?"

Mr. Sánchez tossed his radio inside the van. "Darn things never work up here," he said. Then he turned to Mae and Erin. "Not lost. Missing. There are thousands of miles of backcountry trails. Rangers don't always stay on them."

"He could've surprised a bear," said the guy with the camera.

"Or worse," said his friend.

Mae shuddered. "Worse?"

The leader pulled a snapshot from his pocket. "Keep an eye open," he said.

Erin and Mae studied the picture: the ranger in his uniform, his wife, and two young boys. "How long has he been missing?" Erin asked.

"Three and a half weeks," said Mr. Sánchez. "No sign of him was found in the first ten days so the search efforts were scaled back. They had helicopters and dogs canvassing the mountains."

"Really?" Mae said, eyes wide.

He pocketed the photo and led the Discovery Bound group to the trailhead, strung out in pairs. Erin wondered if taking a bunch of delinquents into the wilderness could rehabilitate them.

Back at the car, Erin traded her sandals for sneakers and tossed an extra pair of socks in her pack. She found garbage bags filled with empty soda cans in the trunk. She dumped them by the spare tire and folded the sticky plastic: Instant rain gear.

"It's steaming hot here," Mae said, batting at bugs. "I'm ready for that swim."

"Me too," Erin said.

Levi took the lead across a grassy field that dipped into a pine forest. Indian paintbrush and monkey flower grew everywhere.

Single file, Erin and Mae followed Levi, jumping from boulder to boulder across shallow streams. Amazingly, no one slipped. The Discovery Bound kids hiked ahead on the same trail, moving faster in spite of their heavy packs.

Erin crossed a sandy margin that looked more like a beach than mountain terrain. Gram had told her that these sandy wastelands were from sheep and cattle overgrazing in the last century. Gram called domestic sheep "hoofed locusts."

"I'm melting." Mae stopped to wipe sweat off her face. "I hope the lake is cold."

Erin rolled her eyes. Obviously, Mae had never swum in an alpine lake. The water would be cold enough to crack her teeth—at least that's how it would feel.

Two miles up the switchback Mae stopped again, pulling out the map. "It didn't look this far on paper."

"It always looks closer on a map than it really is," Erin said. "You have to figure out the scale."

Mae looked up. "What's that?"

"The legend," Levi threw over his shoulder. "An inch on that map is about twenty-five miles. It's four or five miles to the lake."

Mae made a face. "You didn't tell me that."

"You didn't ask."

Mae groaned. "Siberian Outpost. Forgotten Canyon. Bloody Gulch," she said, reading landmarks. "Where do they get these names?"

Erin shrugged, tracking the route with her finger. The trail to Chicken Springs Lake had been darkened with a pencil. "Cottonwood Pass is 11,200 feet. That's only three thousand feet lower than Mt. Whitney," Erin said. "That's the highest mountain in the lower forty-eight."

"You mean forty-eight states?" Mae asked.

"Yeah. Denali in Alaska is taller." Erin glanced up the trail at the drab green packs of the Discovery Bound team. "We shouldn't complain. Not with what those guys are carrying."

Levi stopped to wait at a swift stream. "You two are slower than rocks," he said. He pushed his empty bottle underwater, then lifted it to his mouth.

"Don't drink that!" Erin slapped the bottle away. "That water could have giardia." She dug through her pack, finding a vial of tablets. "Put two of these in your bottle and wait ten minutes. Iodine. It kills microscopic bugs."

Erin added tablets to her own bottle and filled it. She offered some tablets to Mae.

"You always carry that stuff with you?" Mae asked, dropping the iodine into her bottle.

"My grandma insists we carry it in the wilderness in case our water filter breaks," Erin said. "Guess it was still in my pack from my last hike."

Levi smirked. "We should've brought your granny, too."

"You couldn't keep up with her," Erin shot back.

"Come on, Levi, admit it," Mae said. "You would've chugged a bottle of bad bugs if Erin hadn't stopped you. Then you'd—" She turned to Erin. "What would happen?"

"You'd be hatching mosquito eggs in your stomach," Erin said. She didn't know if that could really happen. But it sounded good. "And if you didn't pack toilet paper you'd be stripping leaves off trees."

"Everyone knows about iodine," Levi said with a burp. "No big deal."

"Then why didn't you bring some?" Mae asked.

Levi grunted something that sounded like "Go lose yourself" and started walking.

"Too bad iodine can't make funky water look good," Mae said, spitting out a mouthful. "It even tastes brown."

Erin and Mae turned to the clanking sound of a horseback rider and a pack mule on the trail behind them. The guy reminded Erin of her history teacher, tall and skinny. Duct tape patched the rider's jeans and spurs hugged his leather boots.

The mule's rope was snubbed around the cowboy's saddle horn; the load looked about to break through the blue tarp. A Border collie trotted beside the horse, two red bandannas twisted into a collar.

"How 'bout a lift?" Mae called to him.

He laughed at the joke, then said, "I'm full up with equipment for the search-and-rescue team. I'm hauling kitchen gear to their first camp. They're carrying most of their food and everything else. Their packs must weigh sixty pounds."

"Think they'll find the ranger?" Erin asked.

"They figure he's somewhere within eighty square miles," he said, squinting under the rim of a sweat-stained hat. "We're countin' on them finding him soon. He has a family waiting for him in Ridgecrest and they're gettin' pretty anxious."

Erin thought of the picture with the two young boys. "I wish the rescue team had dogs too."

"Not after three weeks," the cowboy said.

"Why not?" Mae asked.

"You don't want to know, young lady," he said.

"Yes, I do."

The cowboy ignored her. "Name's Jake," he said, giving his horse a kick to spur him up the rocky trail. The mule pulled stubbornly against the rope before following. Jake whistled to his dog. "Come on, Sequoia."

All morning the sky had been a piercing blue. Now clouds were blowing in from the west, gathering in gray bundles. "You think it's gonna rain?" Erin called out, knowing they still had two miles to go.

Jake nodded. "Might need a rain slicker before the day's out," he said.

Erin listened as the metal shoes of the horse and mule clanged against rock. The sound magnified in the mountain air, the echo bouncing off the barren ridges. She and Mae threaded their way up the switchback. It was a lot steeper than it looked from below. Levi hiked a few hundred yards ahead with one of the Discovery Bound kids.

The nearly vertical mountain was studded with pines and rock slides. In the sunny patches, the heat was searing and burned through their shirts. Erin's steps were shorter on the steepest stretches, her feet swinging more freely where the switchback flattened into a turn on the needle-strewn ground.

The eastern slope of the Sierra Nevada was abrupt, a chunk of the earth's crust turned sideways and uplifted along a major fault line. Erin knew it was the largest block of granite on earth. She glanced down the switchback. At 9,000 feet lodgepole pines grew straight and tall. But farther up the trail the trees were smaller. At 10,000 feet they were ground-hugging shrubs.

Miles below, Highway 395 looked like a ribbon sewn into the valley floor. Beyond the highway and stark desert, peaks rose higher than where she stood now, above the 11,000-foot mark. That was the timberline. No trees grew above that mark in these mountains.

Mae stopped to sip her water. "What did Jake mean about the dogs?"

Erin stopped too. "There are all types of search-and-rescue dogs," she said, brushing back sweaty bangs. "Some track by searching out clues on the ground. Others sniff the air. Some are trained in water rescue. But I think he was talking about dogs that specialize in locating bodies. Cadaver dogs."

Mae nearly choked. "You mean dogs that look for dead people?"

"They'll find the ranger soon," Erin said hopefully.

CHAPTER FOUR

It is not the mountains we conquer, but ourselves.
—Sir Edmund Hillary

Erin glanced at the clouds stacking up on the long, narrow ridge above them. Red clusters of Indian paintbrush had disappeared at 8,000 feet. Up this high even low-growing shrubs battled for space between massive granite boulders.

Levi stopped to check on Mae. "Hurry up!" he said. But he didn't wait.

Mae stripped to a tank top. "A little rain would feel good about now," she said when a cloud floated by the sun.

Erin nodded. "And settle the dust."

Mae chattered constantly as they hiked. She covered all her favorite things. "The best night of the week is Wednesday. My parents work late and Levi has band practice. So I have control of the TV remote. My favorite show is *Dream Makeovers*. What's yours?"

Erin shrugged. "We don't have a TV."

"That has to be boring—with a capital B."

After finishing the commentary on her daily routine, Mae asked a lot of questions about Erin's camping trips. "Do you and your grandmother go alone? Do you share a tent? What do you eat? Do your parents ever go?"

Erin was used to questions about Gram. Her new friends at Lee Vining Middle School had asked her why she lived with her grandmother. They were curious about this strange outdoorsy woman who looked nothing like their own grandmas. Erin had learned to change the subject by firing back questions of her own.

She kept an even pace and tried to tune Mae out. Scraps of the girl's life kept filtering in: overprotective parents who wanted her to go to college, plans of her own about going to beauty school, blah-blah-blah. "I mean, what's wrong with wanting to be a hair stylist?" Mae said.

Erin didn't answer.

"Someday I'll have my own salon," Mae insisted.

By the time they passed the biggest ponderosa pine Erin had ever seen, she had heard all about how Mae's mom scooped ice cream at Carlotta's Candy Counter in Crestview and how her dad was a house painter with his own business.

"My guidance counselor thinks beauty school is a great idea," Mae said.

Erin nodded like she cared.

As she settled into a comfortable rhythm, her

mind wandered to the day eleven months ago when she'd found the note from her mom. She'd stood in the hall reading the words on the first page, the letters perfectly formed. Controlled. But on the second page the words were sloppy, as if they didn't know what they wanted to say.

"No!" It had come out as a scared whisper. Erin had read the letter over and over, repeating the words aloud, hearing her mom's voice. "Sorry." Erin wasn't sure what that meant. Sorry for leaving? Sorry for not explaining why she'd left? Sorry for not saying when she was coming back? If she ever would?

Erin wanted to know—and she didn't want to know.

She'd stood in the hall, her feet stuck to the carpet. The walls were falling in around her, squeezing her so tight she couldn't breathe. She felt alone in her sadness. No one was home to notice.

The next morning she'd made a schedule in fifteen-minute time slots. Alarm clock: 6:15 A.M. Breakfast: 6:30. Get dressed: 6:45. Make lunch: 7:00. She'd taken the bus to school, sat through classes, ridden the bus home. Focused on homework. Rarely talked to anyone. She hadn't even told her best friend Carlie that Lannie had left.

Erin had kept the note, going over the words again and again until they blurred. Sometimes the blur put her to sleep. She'd never liked naps, but she started sleeping a lot, even during class. Closing her eyes seemed to keep the sadness in. She'd tried to let it all out a few times, crying and crying. Once she cried so hard she threw up that day's lunch special.

Dad was a mess back then too. He moved through the house in a trance, barely eating, barely talking. He wore the same ratty sweats for days, even though Erin set a clean pair on his bed. He carried the phone everywhere, looking hopeful whenever it rang, then slumping when it wasn't Lannie. Erin was terrified because he was behaving almost like Lannie had right before she left.

Erin and her dad passed the days doing the best they could to take care of each other. They took turns calling friends and relatives. An aunt and uncle in Vermont. Distant cousins scattered across the Southwest. Mom's brother in Nevada, a dishwasher in a casino. No one had heard from Lannie.

In desperation, her dad called the police. Technically, a person wasn't considered "missing" unless foul play was suspected. It wasn't against the law, the officer had pointed out, for an adult to run away from home.

Then one morning her dad shaved early and made waffles for breakfast. "Let's go for a drive," he said and packed lunch in a cooler.

Five hours later Dad and Erin pulled up to the old farmhouse in Lee Vining. Gram hadn't been expecting them, but she didn't seem surprised, either. She flung open the screen door, made a pot of herbal tea, and set out a plate of raisin oatmeal cookies.

Erin and her dad sat side by side in the wooden-slat swing, the one built by Erin's grandpa, who'd died before Erin was born. Erin made little pushes back and forth with her feet. They rocked together quietly on the porch and watched blue jays at the feeder, a pinecone studded with sunflower seeds.

Sometimes they stared straight ahead at nothing.

One day smudged into the next. Erin lost herself by writing poems and turning them into songs. What she liked about writing was the soothing way the words repeated themselves in her head, even after she stopped singing. Words make her feel like a normal kid. Sometimes Erin's songs answered questions she didn't know she was asking.

There had been a few times when she let herself think about her other house and best friends, especially Carlie. She missed everything so much it hurt.

Her dad busied himself in Gram's garden: raking, weeding, pruning. He moved around the twenty-three acres like a wooden chess piece, his face barely changing expressions. He rarely smiled. He didn't talk about Lannie. But he didn't act like everything was okay, either.

Once, while picking worms off a tomato vine, he said, "I'm sorry, Erin. I wish I could be your father and mother."

Erin hugged him hard. "I love you, Dad," she whispered.

The next day he said he had to go out of town. Erin assumed it was for a new photo assignment. He returned six days later and backed the rented moving van up to the porch. She was climbing the stubby oak tree in the front yard.

Erin climbed higher and made herself small, while little explosions went off inside her. She sat on a limb and chewed her knuckles, watching her father unload their old life. When he carted in the last box, she used her pocketknife to carve her initials in the bark of the tree—E. R. She'd hoped the permanence of the scar would make her feel like she belonged. But it only made her feel bad for wounding such a noble tree.

She sat alone in the tree island for a long time, her feet dangling, her arms stiff as branches. Somehow she knew none of the boxes held any of the special things that had belonged to Lannie. Not the onyx jewelry box with the carved angel. Not the scrap of canvas from a Buddhist monastery. Not the neatly folded silk napkin where she set her cup of chamomile tea at night.

One morning she saw her dad standing in the driveway. He was kicking the deep ruts left by the moving van. Erin had watched through the window. Her dad was crying.

CHAPTER FIVE

*Whether adversity be a stumbling block, discipline or
blessing, depends altogether on the use made of it.*
— *ANONYMOUS*

Erin and Mae finally caught up to Levi. Or, Erin
thought, more likely he'd slowed down on the
searing trail and burned out. He sat on a log, eating a protein bar and swigging water from his bottle.
Sweat soaked his shirt.

"If you two were any slower," Levi said. "You'd
be going backwards."

"We didn't want to pass you," Mae tossed out.

Levi chuckled. "Right."

When it started to sprinkle, Erin threw her head
back, welcoming the gentle drops. The lake and its
outlet creek were higher still, beyond the narrow
summit and southwest slopes. There should have
been a breathtaking view of Sequoia National Park
to the west and Death Valley to the east, Erin knew,
but all visibility was lost to a fine mist.

The drizzle turned to gentle rain, painting the sky
a dreary gray. Shadows on the far-reaching peaks
intensified in the lowlands below. Up close the

woods looked like what they were: a crowded group of pines and scrub brush spanning hundreds of thousands of acres.

Not far up the trail, Jake stood by his horse near an outcrop where coarse rocks pushed up through the dry, reddish soil. His full-length slicker flapped as he retied the tarp on the mule's back. He'd already knotted a piece of yellow plastic over Sequoia's back. Erin smiled. It didn't seem like a cowboy thing to do.

The Discovery Bound leader and a few kids huddled near the mule, slipping into their rain slickers. The rest of the group must have already crested the ridge, hiking the last stretch of trail to Chicken Springs Lake.

Erin took the garbage bags from her pack, tearing holes for her head and arms. The rain was steadier now. Fat drops slapped her in the face. She handed the makeshift ponchos to Mae and Levi.

"What're these for?" Levi asked. He wadded up the plastic and crammed it in his pocket.

"It's raining harder," Erin said. "Your clothes won't dry up here."

"Who cares?" he said. "I'm going swimming."

He's right, Erin thought. Why should I care about someone who's stupid and stubborn? She showed Mae how to put on her poncho.

Erin tried to look up through the pine trees to see if there were patches of light sky. Rain pricked her cheeks and seeped inside the plastic. The cloud ceiling was solid, getting darker as she watched. "We should go back," she said.

"Afraid to get wet?" Levi asked.

"Maybe it won't last long," Mae said to Erin.

"Maybe," Erin said, but the weather didn't show any signs of clearing. If anything, the rain was coming down harder. "We shouldn't take a chance, though. We don't have any gear."

Levi glanced back at Erin. "It's just a cloudburst, then it'll be hot as ever," he said. "But you're right. You two should go back. Wait in the car. Listen to music. I'll see you after my swim."

Erin was about to tell him to take a hike when the mountain exploded.

A fist of thunder grabbed the ridge and shook it.

Lightning split the sky.

It started to hail, ice the size of frozen peas.

The hailstones started falling harder and faster, bullets of ice ricocheting off trees and boulders. Erin shielded her face from the ice and hunkered by a fat tree trunk for protection. Mae hunched beside her, trembling in her makeshift poncho. Levi, already soaked, scrambled to put his on.

Within minutes the peas were the size of walnuts: thousands of ice balls hitting the ground and bouncing higher than their heads. Hail hammered them, an ice shower on full force. Higher up, beyond the rock outcrop, a tree crashed down in a torrent of red mud.

Erin watched the mule freak out. It stumbled

backwards, eyes bulging, mouth frothing. Jake twisted in his saddle, struggling not to let go of the lead rope. The wet rope and his gloves were slick as oil. The mule kept pulling, the gear on its back slipping sideways.

Erin forced herself to stand up, wondering if she could help. Under another blinding bolt of lightning, Mr. Sánchez rushed over to the mule and slapped it on the rump. The mule pitched forward, one step, then two.

"Get down!" Jake shouted to Erin, Mae, and Levi. "Lightning goes for the tallest trees—or what's near them!"

A zigzag of white whips cracked the air.

Erin squatted on her heels, hugging her knees.

When the next bolt struck a boulder, Jake's slicker lit up as if by a powerful spotlight. A tree groaned. Someone up ahead shrieked. The horse neighed, a long, high-pitched squeal. The mule shook so hard the kitchen gear under the sagging tarp rattled.

Erin tugged on Mae's poncho. "Come on, we have to get off the ridge!" she yelled over the storm. "Or we're dead!"

CHAPTER SIX

There are some things you learn best in calm, and some in storm.
—WILLA CATHER

Erin stood up and reached for Mae's hand, then fell back when another flash lit up the ridge. The hail had slackened, but it was raining hard now. The trail was almost impassible, engulfed in a muddy torrent.

Lightning crackled along the mineral-rich ridge.

Thunder rumbled over them.

"The earth is splitting open!" Erin heard one of the Discovery Bound kids cry.

Near the outcrop, another kid cowered under a tree. "We're gonna be swallowed whole!"

"We have to get away from the trees!" Erin shouted a warning to anyone who could hear. "They're all lightning rods!"

Mae started to move, but a jagged bolt stopped her. She leaned against a trunk, a thick-barked monster. A nearby tree fell with a deep, throaty wail. Erin and Mae crouched lower, pulling the poncho over their heads as if that could save them from the falling giants. The claws of wind and hail ripped through the plastic.

Mae fell to her knees. "Please don't let us die up here!" she moaned.

Crash! Another tree down.

Erin thought she heard a scream. She forced herself to look up. Less than fifty feet away, the blue tarp on the mule's back flashed as a jag of lightning struck it. The mule shimmied, then fell over. The horse reared, its eyes bulging, and threw Jake from the saddle. Then the riderless horse stumbled sideways, dropped to its knees, and went all the way down.

Trembling, Erin took in the horrible scene. "No!" she cried. Her eyes searched the trail for Jake's yellow slicker.

"Jake!" she hollered.

No answer.

What had happened to him?

Erin saw the horse raise its head and whinny, then drop its muzzle in the raging water. The mule never moved. The lead rope was still wound limply around the saddle horn. Erin started to cry. She couldn't help it. Her eyes burned from wind and icy rain and tears. She cried for the horse and mule. "This can't be happening..." she whispered.

All she could see were two dead animals and endless trees. "Jake!"

The storm didn't show any signs of loosening its grip.

Lightning hammered the ridge.

Thunder boomed.

"I don't wanna die..." Mae muttered helplessly.

Levi slowly rose, shouting above the storm. "That guy needs help!" he called to Erin and Mae.

Mae clutched his poncho.

Levi pulled free. "He might be hurt."

Erin drew in a breath, slowly getting to her feet, wishing she'd seen this side of Levi earlier. "I'll go with you."

"Come on," he said.

Levi and Erin picked their way through the trees.

Mae hesitated, then followed, shrinking at every glaring flash.

Erin stopped, listening. "Did you hear that?" she asked.

Mae shook her head.

Levi pushed ahead through rivers of mud.

The thunder ricocheting off the ridge was nearly deafening.

Then Erin heard it again.

"Help!"

Erin recognized Jake's voice, but she couldn't see him.

"Somebody help me!" he screamed again.

Erin rushed in the direction of his cries.

Mae slipped but didn't go all the way down.

Erin scrambled back and gave her a hand.

When she felt sure that Mae was all right, Erin

looked back. She took one step and froze. Mr. Sánchez was stumbling around in a scattering of pines, dazed. Black burn marks etched his face, jagged like lightning bolts, a sign he'd been struck. Smoke curled from his hair. Even through the rain she could smell the burning stench. Sickening. Two kids tried to steady him.

Another kid was sprawled face down in the gushing trail, his arm twisted at a weird angle. He was stunned, barely conscious. Levi helped lift the heavy pack off his back, rolled him over, and cleaned out his mouth. Otherwise the kid would've choked to death on mud.

Erin felt stunned herself. She didn't know what to do. Jake screamed again, louder. "Help! I'm trapped!" His voice was a mixture of pain and panic.

Terror-stricken, she turned and saw Jake for the first time. He was tangled under the dead horse, his expression wild with fear. Two of the Discovery Bound kids kneeled beside him, talking in low voices. Jake let out an agonizing cry.

Erin squeezed her eyes shut. This was bad. Real bad.

She tried to think but it was achingly hard. The cold had started to eat into her bones. All she could think of was the lightning; all she could hear was the roll of thunder. And Jake screaming.

The town of Lone Pine wasn't that far away, Erin knew. It had a hospital. Doctors specializing in wilderness trauma, like lightning strikes. But from where they were right now, Lone Pine might as well be on another planet.

Mae caught up to her as another boom rumbled across the mountains. She stared at the horse and mule and their open, unseeing eyes stared back. For a moment the mountain was mute. Then, another roar of thunder shook the ground under them.

Mae screamed and ran.

"Mae!" Erin called after her. "Come back!"

Mae didn't slow down.

"Mae!" Levi yelled and started after her. Erin saw him trip on a root and twist his ankle. "Go after her!" he pleaded, drawing his leg up in pain.

Erin hesitated.

"Go on!"

She took off.

The mountain's spine made a bend where a sudden gush of rust-colored water tumbled into a foggy mist. Erin spotted Mae a hundred yards below on the western slope. She was on the wrong side of the mountain—the slope opposite the trail to Horseshoe Meadows.

"Mae!" Erin called. She headed down after her. "You're going the wrong way!"

The west side was a maze of swift-flowing streams. Countless gulches ran reddish-brown from the downpour. Lightning hurled its fiery fists, beating the clouds. Bright flashes chased Mae down the ridge. Thunder cracked. It was close. Too close. The air was thick, charged with electricity.

Erin dove headfirst into a patch of brush. The wiry branches scratched her face. Stay low, she told herself, tossing her watch because of the metal band. She clutched her earrings. Angels. They matched the onyx jewelry box. She took them off and shoved them deep in her pocket. She'd never catch Mae at this rate.

"Mae!" she yelled again, her cupped hands a megaphone. She turned in the direction she guessed Mae had gone. She yelled until her throat ached, her head ached, everything ached.

She rushed on, stumbling blindly. Her braid was long gone. Corkscrew hair plastered her face. She called again and stopped to listen. "Mae!" She barely heard her own voice.

Stay calm, she told herself. What a stupid thing to say, she thought. How could she be calm?

Farther down the slope she counted the seconds between a flash of lightning and the next roll of thunder. "One-one thousand…" She could judge the distance of a storm this way, roughly figuring one second for each one thousand she counted. "…ten-one thousand…" Fifteen seconds passed. The storm was around three miles away, probably still attacking the pass.

Was Mae on the ridge? Erin had no way of knowing. No trails remained anywhere. Just rivers of swirling mud. Erin tried not to think about what she would tell Mae when she found her. Taking off like that? Insane!

She picked her way around tangles of brush, trying to sort out what had happened on the trail. The mule had taken a direct hit with all that metal on its back, kitchen gear for the Discovery Bound group. The lightning could have bounced off the metal, striking the leader. Or it could have traveled along the ground, a river of high-voltage electricity.

Then she remembered: the horse and mule were wearing metal shoes. They didn't stand a chance. And poor Jake, trapped. If the group worked together using ropes, she thought, they could drag the horse off him.

Erin scanned the forest. She could see about twenty feet in some directions, depending on the denseness of the trees. She tried to quicken her pace on the flatter ground, but kept tripping on mud-covered rocks and roots. When the slope fanned out, she stopped, trying to figure out how long it had been since she'd seen Mae.

She glanced over her shoulder, half-expecting to see Levi. Impossible, she knew, especially if he had sprained his ankle.

"Mae!" she yelled again. Hearing no response between the claps of thunder, Erin pushed on.

Gram had once described the making of summer thunderheads. The desert floor acts like a burner under a pan of water, sending moist air into a cold lid. "One lightning bolt can have millions of volts," she'd said.

Erin scrambled around another bend, facing a downed tree too fat to climb over, too low to wiggle underneath. Mae couldn't have come this way, she thought, unless she went around the tree. Which way would she go from there?

You've already lost her, a voice scolded in her head.

Erin dropped to her knees. Blinking against the rain, she saw a hollow near the root side of the trunk. It looked as if the ground around the opening had been recently disturbed. Maybe Mae had come this way. Erin wiggled through, got to her feet and stumbled on. Every time she took a step, she felt more water seep into her shoes. Why hadn't she worn hiking boots? Then she remembered. Sneakers were perfectly good for a two-week stay in Camarillo.

She recalled Gram telling her about a storm a few years ago when sixty inches of rain were dumped on the Sierra Nevada in two months. The rains were warm, causing the heaviest run-off in thirty years. Flash floods had knocked out roads, trails, bridges, power poles. Then temperatures had dipped below freezing. No electricity meant no heat. Gram liked to point out the twenty-mile stretch of highway that had suffered a hundred landslides. "Sirens from those emergency vehicles wailed all night," she'd told Erin.

Was this that kind of rain? Erin wondered, scanning trees around a meadow alive with summer wildflowers. She suddenly stopped and spun around. From the corner of her eye she spotted movement. The brownish lump was out of place, too big.

Quiet! she told herself, startled. It could be a bear.

Ursus americanus rarely attacked people, she knew, but you had to be careful. Erin stared at the clearing, gripping the straps of her pack. She swiveled slowly, letting her eyes rest on shapes, searching for something that didn't belong.

"Bears like to charge," Gram had said, "but it's usually a bluff. If a bear charges, make yourself look big by opening your jacket and raising your arms. If that doesn't work, drop face down, tuck in a ball, and clutch the back of your neck."

Then she saw it: A large mule deer, reddish brown. Relieved, Erin let herself breathe. It raised its head, looking here and there, showing off forked antlers. Beautiful.

A jag of lightning turned the air white. Up the slope a dead tree burst into flames. The buck bolted in a stiff-legged gait and disappeared in the trees. Thunder boomed on the ridge.

"Mae!" Erin cried desperately.

She staggered on.

CHAPTER SEVEN

To me a lush carpet of pine needles or spongy grass
is more welcome than the most luxurious Persian rug.
—HELEN KELLER

Erin zigzagged through the trees, checking the area around her for Mae. She slowed at another uprooted tree as the sun broke through the clouds. Steam rose from the ground, seeping under her poncho, mixing with nervous sweat. The waistband of Erin's wet shorts chafed her skin.

She glanced up a side canyon that looked like a giant rock drain. Red water gushed down from all sides, tumbling into a deep ravine.

Erin set a steady pace in spite of being cold, wet, and weary. She had to find Mae. Time was running out.

Soon darkness would claim the mountains.

She pushed through puddles, looking for footprints. Once she thought she spotted a fresh print, but in all the mud, it was hard to tell. She kept on, every step moving her further from Cottonwood Pass and Horseshoe Meadows and away from her home in Lee Vining.

Finally, Erin spotted Mae through a sparse stand of foxtail pines. Erin splashed through mud holes, crawled over fallen trees, her sneakers crushing pinecones. Muck caked her soles, making every step awkward. Bushes attacked her bare legs. She wondered if she'd ever make it through.

Mae sat slumped on a rotting log, a tiny figure in a garbage bag with only her eyes peering out. She looked confused, like she was in a bad dream and couldn't wake up.

Erin sank to the log, worn-out.

"The guy on the ground," Mae said, shaking like crazy. "The poor horse."

Erin pulled a sweatshirt from Mae's pack. "We have to dry out," she said, shedding her own poncho now that the rain had stopped.

"The mule…"

Mae was panting, her cloud breaths fogging the air. Erin couldn't tell if it was from cold or fear or exhaustion. "It could've been so much worse," she said.

"How?" Mae asked.

Erin didn't know. And she didn't know what kind of shape Jake and Mr. Sánchez were in. She told herself the kids must have moved the dead horse off Jake by now.

Mae looked up. "Where's Levi?"

"He wanted to come after you," Erin said. "He twisted his ankle—he'll be okay."

Erin rummaged through her pack and handed Mae half of her squashed peanut butter and honey sandwich. "Eat this."

Mae nodded in the shadowy light.

The two of them ate in silence: cold, shaking, scared.

The sky to the west was a flame of golds and purples. Much too soon daylight would be lost to shadows from the higher peaks. Erin knew how to make a lean-to good enough for one night in the mountains, but she realized they couldn't wait until dark to get started.

"We have to build a fire," she said, even though it seemed impossible with everything so wet. "And make a shelter."

Mae stiffened. "I'm not staying here."

"We can't go anywhere now. It's getting dark."

"But we have to get back!"

Erin started to lose it. "You don't get it, do you? You ran down the mountain for hours. It'd take twice as long to hike back up. Maybe longer."

"What about my brother?" Mae said.

"Levi is with the Discovery Bound group. They have sleeping bags, tents, stoves, food." She cringed, visualizing unpacking the dead mule. "You shouldn't have run away like that."

Mae stared at her mud-soaked sneakers. "Sorry."

"Sorry?" Erin hated that word. It was meaningless. Empty. "What good is that?"

"Don't yell at me," Mae said.

Erin pulled herself together. She grabbed her bike pants from her pack and threw them at Mae. "Put these on."

Mae threw them back. "I have my own pants."

"Fine."

Erin sucked in a deep breath and studied the wood on the ground. It was too wet to light a fire. She found a log that was partially torn apart, probably by a bear looking for carpenter ants.

Using her knife, she stripped away the outer bark and trimmed it to the dry center. The wood fiber could be used for tinder. She found some moss on the underside of a boulder and scraped it off—it would catch quickly too. Mae put on a pair of baggy jeans.

"Look down in those rock crevasses for dry pinecones," Erin said.

"Dry?" Mae asked. "Are you kidding?"

"Would you just look?"

"Okay. Okay." Mae ran her fingers under a low ledge, collecting a handful of fairly dry pine needles and a few cones.

Working kept the two girls warm, although their sneakers were soaked. They'd packed extra clothes, but no shoes.

"Sounds like you and your grandmother camp a lot," Mae said.

"Some," Erin answered.

Mae looked worried. "Wrong answer."

"Lots of people camp. Millions, probably," Erin said. "Here's the difference: When I'm with Gram we have a tent and gear and enough food to feed a family of bears." She shuddered on the word bear, grateful the animal in the meadow had been a deer.

Erin dumped moss on a flat rock and made a tepee with sticks. Tinder and pine needles went on next. She shoved the needles under the tepee, then took a film canister from her pack. Inside were wooden matches, a scrap of sandpaper, and a re-lighting birthday candle.

"Was all that stuff your grandmother's idea too?"

Erin struck a match. "Yeah."

The moss burned up so quickly nothing else caught.

Erin felt like crying.

She forced herself to repeat the process. This time she split sticks and added pine knots and bits of moss, all useful fuel in wet weather. The fire caught, barely. She built it up slowly and added the fire block she'd whittled from the log. Then she put the rest of the wood fiber in one of her extra socks to use later.

"I've never slept outside before," Mae said.

Erin noticed the purple streaks had washed from Mae's hair. "Never?"

"Just once," Mae muttered. "But it was in our backyard. Levi was with me. I ran down the batteries in the flashlight because I was afraid of the dark. I still am. Your turn."

"What?"

"Tell me something you've never done before," Mae said, as if talking would keep them from thinking about the mess they were in.

Erin shrugged. "Jogged in a garbage bag."

"Be serious. You know what I mean."

Erin fed split sticks to the fire and blew on the coals to keep them flaming. When the smaller sticks caught, she added bigger ones. Then she pulled down a dead branch lodged in a tree. Anything to keep the fire alive for the night. "Okay. I never hitchhiked before," she said.

Mae played with a tube of lipstick. "My parents are going to kill me," she said. "Levi and I promised we'd be home before dark."

Erin thought about who was waiting for her. Not Gram. She was still in Bodie. Lannie at the bus station? Probably. But Erin was more concerned about Jake and the leader. And about getting through the night with this airhead.

"I'll tell you another thing," she said. "We broke all the basic rules of hiking: Stay together. If lost, stay in one place. Leave signs for a search party. Never leave someone who's hurt.'"

Mae frowned. "Hiking has rules?"

"Yeah."

Erin looked around. They needed protection from wind and rain. Their shelter should be away from standing dead trees and any rocks uphill that could tumble down in the night. If the wind didn't blow too hard—if a dead tree didn't fall over—if an avalanche of rocks didn't crush them, she thought they'd be okay.

By firelight they dragged rain-soaked branches to a boulder and shook them to get some of the water off. Erin showed Mae how to make a low slanted roof, sort of a half-tent, by propping the branches up against the boulder. Together they worked at overlapping pine boughs to weave a bed, then dragged it into the shelter.

"Drape a garbage bag over the branches," Erin said. "Like a ground cloth."

Mae spread out the plastic the best she could. "We even have another one for a top sheet," she said.

"No, the other bag has to go overhead," Erin said. "In case of more rain." She pulled the corners as tight as possible to keep pockets of water from collecting and weighing down the roof.

"Guess we take turns watching the fire," Mae said. "We wouldn't want to start a forest fire."

"In this swamp?" Erin nearly laughed. "What would burn?"

Mae shrugged.

Listening to the unsettling night sounds, they gathered a few more dry pinecones and crawled in the shelter to begin the long wait for daylight.

CHAPTER EIGHT

Adopt the pace of nature: Her secret is patience.
— RALPH WALDO EMERSON

Erin slept the best she could on a garbage bag spread on pine branches. Every hour or so she woke up feeling scared, unsure where she was. Then she groaned, haunted by the memory of Jake's painful cries.

She rolled over, stiff as a ramrod. Her first instinct was to check the fire, make sure it was still burning. The night air was heavy with its own wet weight. The garbage bag was as muddy as everything else. Erin crawled from the shelter, her skin sticking to the plastic.

Thankfully, the fire still had coals. She pushed a burning branch further into the smoldering embers. Gram called it the shove-and-burn method. Then she crept back into the shelter, listening to the night sounds, watching the clouds eat the starry sky bit by bit. Beside her, Mae's breathing was slow and even. Sometimes she murmured unintelligible words without waking.

* * *

Shortly before dawn the temperature took a sudden drop. Erin awoke to sharp cold stinging her cheeks. Her body ached from lying on the uneven branches. Her neck was stiff; the arm she'd been sleeping on, numb. It felt as if she hadn't had any rest at all.

Erin returned to the fire and tossed pinecones into the flames. Her face was scorching from the heat but her back was an icicle.

Usually a fire made her feel like singing. Gram had taught her songs about donkeys working in gold mines and orphans laying railroad tracks. Erin liked songs about the past. She wondered why teachers didn't use music in class. If kids heard songs with history in them maybe they'd remember names and dates better.

Erin sat by the fire, poking at coals with a long stick. In the resiny glow she imagined the bus rolling into Camarillo. Would Lannie have called Gram's house when she didn't show up? Erin hoped so. She wanted Lannie to worry as much as she had the last eleven months.

Gram wouldn't be home to answer. She'd still be in Bodie with her friends, helping to pick up trash. Playing dominoes with park rangers by the light of a campfire, leading them in songs. Cooking cocoa and popcorn over a butane burner. Later, she'd be warm in her sleeping bag.

Erin thought about trying to gather some rose hips and steeping tea. Hot tea would warm them. But she didn't have a container for boiling water. Besides, it was too early for the best rose hips. They didn't soften until after the first frost.

If Gram were here she'd have already collected pine nuts and pounded them into cakes. Then she would have wrapped the cakes in skunk cabbage leaves and baked them in ashes.

Erin found homemade granola bars and dried apricots in her lunch sack. Thanks, Gram, she thought.

She searched her pack to see what might have been left from another trip. Bug juice, a partial roll of toilet paper, biodegradable shampoo, all in a zip-lock bag. A few more wooden matches and the re-lighting birthday candle in the film canister. Plus her pocketknife: two blades, a screwdriver, a file, and an odd-shaped gadget that opened cans.

Clouds broke up on the horizon and the sky lightened. Erin wiggled her toes inside her shoes to keep the circulation moving. A pool of water at her feet reflected the rock-based fire. "Hey? You going to sleep all day?" she called.

Mae rustled on the garbage bag. "I'm cold."

"We have a fire."

"When will it be morning?"

"It is morning," Erin said. "It's just shady until the sun's higher."

Mae crawled out of the shelter.

"Do you have the map?" Erin asked.

Mae nodded and pulled it out of her pack.

Erin traced the route they had followed yesterday before the storm hit, from Horseshoe Meadows up the east side of the mountain to Cottonwood Pass. The storm had battered the ridge less than a mile from Chicken Spring Lake. She noted a warning stamped on the map: Wood campfires prohibited within 300 feet of water. What a joke! Pools of water surrounded their meager campfire.

Studying the map confirmed what Erin had feared. They were much too far from the ridge to attempt to climb back and join the others. She didn't look forward to telling Mae that they wouldn't be returning to Cottonwood Pass.

"Where were we yesterday?" Mae asked, peering at the map.

Erin showed her, following brown contour lines with her finger. "Now we're here, near this meadow."

Above the green tract, massive plugs of granite formed the peaks of the Sierra Nevada. And farther still, rising from the timberline, a trail angled toward a gap in the crest. It made a series of hairpin turns and veered south before dropping to Horseshoe Meadows.

Erin decided to spit out the bad news. "No one will be on the ridge," she said. "The group would've rigged stretchers for Jake and the leader. The kids would have carried them down the switchback."

"Levi wouldn't go with them," Mae said. "He'd be looking for us...for me."

"Not if he sprained his ankle."

Mae angrily shoved clothes in her knapsack. "I'm going to find my brother."

"Look, Mae. Here's the deal. We don't have enough food to hike up the mountain and down the other side in one day," Erin said, frustrated and exhausted.

Mae faced her. "What are you saying?"

"On an average trail we could hike two miles an hour," Erin tried to explain. "Add another hour for every thousand feet we hike up. But this terrain isn't exactly average. It's a lot tougher. Besides—"

Mae cut her off. "Then I'll go alone."

"Listen to me," Erin argued. "We can hike to the Pacific Crest Trail, then follow it to Sequoia National Park. It'll be full of hikers this time of year. They'll have food and—"

"Forget it. I want to find my brother."

"Someone in the park will have a cell phone. We can call the ranger's station and get help."

"Phones don't work out here," Mae said. "Remember?"

"No one's on that ridge now except a dead horse and mule." Erin's words hung like smoke in the air.

"Levi will be there. I know he will."

"Why would he wait for us?" Erin asked. "He would've figured we headed to the campgrounds. Back to the car. It's a tough hike and we don't have much food."

Mae swung on her pack. "Bet you have badges for all this survival stuff," she said. "Reading maps and building fires."

"Whatever."

Erin used a stick to sweep live embers off the rock. They sizzled and died on the wet ground. "Levi wasn't the one who ran off," she said.

"So the whole storm's my fault?"

There was no use trying to talk sense into Mae. She was the most stubborn person Erin had ever met.

Erin twisted her tangled hair into a lopsided knot, fastening it with a twig. She knew she couldn't let Mae go alone. Mae would never find her way out. Erin hated being bullied into something that felt so wrong. But what choice did she have?

By the time Erin had changed into cutoffs and charted a new route, the sun was beginning to warm the air on their side of the mountain. They hiked wearily up the slope, their shoulders slumped under their packs. Their sneakers, dried overnight by the fire, were muddy again within minutes. Sweat mixed with mud streaked their face and arms and moods.

"If we stay together..." Erin muttered to herself, "...we might have a chance."

The vast sand-rimmed expanse of a meadow below contrasted with the dark green forests around it. Behind them the snowy crags of the Great Western Divide, a chain of mountains running between two major rivers, appeared on the western skyline. Minutes slipped into hours. Neither of them spoke.

Mushrooms seemed to have popped up everywhere overnight, perfect little caps studded with dirt and pine needles. Erin licked her chapped lips. Mushrooms. Sautéed in olive oil, marinated in Italian salad dressing. Every Sunday night Gram stuffed mushrooms with bread crumbs and grated cheese and slid them under the broiler.

Gram knew how to test mushrooms to see if they were safe to eat. Sure, Erin was hungry. But she couldn't remember if a skin that peeled off easily meant they were poisonous toadstools or not. She was not going to be a guinea pig in a deadly guessing game.

Gram always packed a feast on their camping trips. Not those freeze-dried meals in packages. Mexican spoon bread with corn, chili, and cheese baked in a Dutch oven and set deep in a bed of hot coals was her specialty.

Erin led the way into a boulder-choked ravine, then half-crawled up a steep slope littered with shavings of thin rock, weathered and broken. An occasional boulder, stained deep gray, perched on top of the bedrock. The only sound was the constant crunch beneath their shoes, like stepping on broken glass.

Above them a pair of vultures drifted on the air currents. Erin shivered, thinking about the horse and mule. The missing ranger would see the winged clean-up crew, too, if he was in the open. She shook away her dismal thoughts.

Erin and Mae crossed a swag below a massive spike of granite that formed endless peaks. The sun bathed the landscape in a glow that made everything—the sweeping boulders, the irregular outline of pines, and the wispy clouds sailing by—look like a postcard.

"I think that's the Kaweah Peaks Ridge," Erin said. She ate a few dried apricots and passed the bag to Mae. "My dad would know just how to capture it."

"Is he an artist?" Mae asked. She offered Erin some potato chips from her pack.

"A photographer—in South America on assignment."

"You should've gone with him," Mae said.

"You should've picked a lake closer to the road," Erin shot back.

Mae looked miserable. "I guess so."

Ahead a shallow pool was banked with stones black with algae. Erin knelt down, sweat rolling down her back. The skin on her legs was encrusted with rust-red mud. She held her bottle underwater.

"Are we on the same ridge as yesterday?" Mae asked.

There was no sense lying. "I'm not sure."

Mae let her pack drop too. "We're never going to get out of here."

"Sure we will," Erin said. "Just put one foot in front of the other, remember?"

"Yeah." Mae's voice was hollow.

Erin stared unsteadily down the incline they had just hiked up. Countless trees still smoked from lightning strikes. The sky was just as clear as when they'd started out yesterday. Everything can change so quickly, she thought, adding tablets to her water bottle.

Erin set her bottle aside and washed mud off her legs. Mae did the same. The icy water raised goose bumps on their skin. When Erin figured enough time had passed, she shook the bottle and drank more than she should. It made her feel full and bloated.

"If that's the Kaweah Ridge," Erin said, scanning peaks rising on the other side of an expansive valley. "We've gone too far north. Too far west. We should've been looking back more often. Keeping track of meadows, prominent ridges."

"So why weren't we?" Mae asked.

Erin's patience hit a wall. For an instant she wished she'd let Mae hike on her own. She glanced at the sinking sun and rubbed her bare wrist. She wished she hadn't tossed her watch. Mae still wore hers. But Erin didn't want to talk to her. How much daylight is left? she wondered. The sun made a burst of light on the tip of the tallest tree on the ridge. Three o'clock, she figured. Or close enough. They had maybe four more hours of good light.

The trail was practically straight up the steep face of fine-grained rock. Erin led the way up the slope, crunching over piles of broken glacier rock. The rain had left patches that were slick as oil. They stopped and started a dozen times before reaching a rocky saddle.

Mae stared at the desolate-looking landscape, her eyes wavering between fear and self-pity. "Everything looks the same."

Erin shivered as a light wind blew past, her clothes clammy with sweat. They were on a ridge. That was obvious. The vista was far-reaching, the rocks solid sculptures. Millions of trees. But no smoke from campfires. No sign of trails. Not even the beaten paths animals made.

She leaned over the cliff edge. Dislodged pebbles cascaded in a rocky stream down the wall. She had no idea where they were in relationship to Cottonwood Pass.

Suddenly Erin thought about her dad, knowing how worried he'd be if he knew she was lost in the mountains. These days she stayed connected to him through long-distance phone calls, oversized post-cards, and his photographs in magazines. Some of them showed girls her age. They were always smil-ing. Maybe it was her dad's way of willing happiness for her. She kept wishing he'd take assignments closer to home. But the magazine already had a photographer in California.

Then her thoughts turned to Gram. Gram would be able to take her by the hand and lead her out. She remembered something she'd read in an outdoor magazine once: When you're lost, any direction you choose is the wrong one. When you keep going, you only become more lost.

Erin suddenly felt lightheaded. She dropped down onto a boulder.

Mae turned toward the massive pinnacles, then stumbled backwards as if the worst thought in the world had just slugged her in the gut. "Do you think this is how that ranger got lost?"

Erin rubbed her neck to ease the dull pain.

"He's *missing*," she corrected.

CHAPTER NINE

The important thing for you is not how much you know,
but the quality of what you know.
—ERASMUS

Erin stood up wearily. She wobbled slightly as Mae's words replayed in her head. *Is this what happened to that ranger?*

We have to stay positive, Erin told herself. Or we're doomed.

Mae's gaze darted over the mountains. "Levi!" she called into empty air.

Erin trembled as a light wind blew past, her clothes clammy with sweat. She chugged on her water bottle. It smelled like stale gym socks. Maybe if she gulped loud enough, it would blot out other sounds, like the rumbling in her stomach. She hated being reminded that they'd been out here so long.

For the first night of camping Gram always packed chicken breasts, marinating them in barbecue sauce in two tin cups. They used the cups later for oatmeal or soup. Gram would skewer the meat on twigs and set them on the edge of the fire so the skin wouldn't burn. The fat in the chicken skin made the fire sputter and spit.

Erin was grateful for the dried fruit and potato chips, but right now she and Mae needed something more nourishing.

Mae slumped down on a boulder. "I wonder why they haven't found the ranger."

"Someone may have by now," Erin said, trying to sound calm. She pushed back her hair, a curtain of tangles. "But you heard what Jake said. They narrowed the area to eighty square miles. That's still a lot of terrain. And it's just as rugged as it was in Muir's day more than a hundred years ago."

"Will they send out someone to search for us?" Mae asked.

"Eventually, I guess. But I doubt that anyone with the Discovery Bound group is worrying about us right now."

"Levi won't give up," Mae said.

Erin didn't answer. She didn't like the look of the clouds drifting in over the mountains. Lightning only needed two things: moist air and sun-heated surfaces, like boulders. She scanned the rocky spine, retracing their steps in her head and trying to figure out where they'd gone wrong. It was impossible to count all the times they'd backtracked to get around thorny clumps of brush and impassable gullies.

"Did you see that?" Mae asked suddenly.

Erin followed Mae's gaze over a group of straggly treetops. The trees had been snapped off six feet above ground, probably by an avalanche. "What?"

"Something yellow," Mae said. "Above those broken trees."

Erin shaded her eyes. Across the valley to the west, halfway up the saddle about a quarter of a mile away she thought she saw something move. It was smaller than a bear, bigger than a raccoon. "Maybe it's a hiker."

"Come on!" Mae said, jumping up.

Erin called, "Wait!" She couldn't believe how quickly Mae could move when she had a good reason. She followed the blond girl down the slope, her eyes searching for the bit of color. Her throat felt thick, her lips flaky. Her head pounded. Dehydration, probably.

Halfway down they stopped to catch their breath. "Where's the yellow thing?" Mae asked.

"I don't know." Erin rubbed her stomach. "You have anything else to eat?"

"Nothing but chips." Mae wormed out of her knapsack. "You can have them. I'm not hungry anyway."

Erin was worried about Mae. Her lack of hunger could be a sign of dehydration. They were both exhausted and they hadn't had nearly enough water for such a hot day. Although late afternoon shadows had begun moving into the valley, the temperature still boiled. There must be a rule for how much water a person needed when hiking in searing heat. Whatever it was, Erin didn't know it. But even if they had water, it would be impossible for them to carry enough to keep hydrated.

Erin thought about the river that cut through the valley floor. According to the map, it was a fork of the Kern. They needed to get to water and forget about this yellow thing. It was probably nothing anyway.

Mae had shed her sweatshirt hours ago. Her tank top was so wet it looked like she'd been swimming. Her cheeks were streaked with reddish-brown mud. Erin knew she probably looked even more pitiful.

"Come on," she said, handing Mae her pack. "Let's go. It's not that far to the stream."

Without a word Mae shouldered the backpack and followed her. In half an hour they could hear the running water. It only took them a little longer to reach a spot where a huge tree next to the stream had uprooted, leaving a small clearing among the rocks.

"We can get water here, but first we have to build a signal fire," Erin said.

"We can't stop now. What if that was a hiker?"

"Then he'll see the smoke."

"Why would a hiker notice that?" Mae asked. "People always have fires when they camp."

"Not in the heat of the day."

"But—" Mae started.

Erin glared at her. "But *what?*"

Mae backed down.

Erin rummaged in the pocket of her pack and

pulled out the extra sock she'd filled with dry wood fiber. This time it didn't take her long to start a fire on the rocky riverbank. After it was going strong she and Mae added a wet log. The fire hissed and the smoke turned thick and black.

Erin grabbed her pack and walked to the river. She stripped to her sports bra and squeezed a glob of toothpaste on her finger. The cool peppermint taste soothed her parched mouth. "Wash area downstream," she called to Mae. "Drinking water upstream."

"Is that another rule?" asked Mae, picking her way over the rocks to the water's edge.

Erin rubbed her teeth with her finger and tossed the toothpaste to Mae. "Even animals don't drink their own bath water."

Mae washed her face and splashed water on her neck, then stood air-drying in the sun. "Well, I can't stay here doing nothing," she said, "when there might be someone out there who can help us."

"We built a fire," Erin said. "Now we're waiting to see if anyone spots the smoke."

"I wish we had something to cook over the fire," Mae said dully. "That ranger probably starved to death."

"Rangers always pack a ton of food. Besides, they know what's safe to eat in the wilderness," Erin said. "Gram makes soup, bread, even pudding from the mealy flour of acorns. She wraps the dough in fern leaves and bakes it in hot ashes."

"Where is your grandmother when we need her?" Mae sighed.

"Camping with friends right now." For a second Erin thought she caught a whiff of roasted chicken. Her mouth even watered. Was she losing it?

"Sounds like you spend a lot of time with her."

"Well..." Erin said slowly. "I live with her."

Mae didn't say anything for a while. Then she looked at Erin with a puzzled expression. "Where's your mom?"

"She left last year."

"How come?"

Mae's constant questions were as annoying as a fly buzzing around Erin's head. She felt like swatting her.

Erin swallowed her reply and sat in a circle of roots that made a kind of chair under a buckeye tree. She began to throw pebbles in the river. Not to make a splash, but to send Mae a message that she didn't want to talk about Lannie.

"I'm always getting grounded for stupid small stuff," Mae said. "Not like getting lost. That's big-time stupid."

Erin hated to admit it, but for once Mae had a point. "We're stuck out here another night, I guess."

Mae looked beaten.

Erin glanced around. The tree had fallen into the river, its roots weakened where water eroded the bank. The river would have been swollen with snowmelt in spring, she knew, hurling water against the banks. Now it only boiled white where it tumbled over rocks.

Erin stood up and brushed dirt from her butt. Daylight had passed much too quickly. She traded her cutoffs for long pants and pulled a sweatshirt over her tank top. Her socks were stiff with mud, but she left them on. Blisters would be the kiss of death.

The girls collected wood and pinecones and stacked them by the fire. They had no trouble finding branches to build another lean-to under the fallen tree. Then they turned their pockets inside out and put together a dinner of stale Gummy Bears and broken potato chips. Mae had a starved expression on her face as she guzzled water and greedily licked her fingers.

"What I'd give for a chocolate shake," Mae said.

"Pizza—extra large," Erin tossed in glumly.

"Too bad phones don't work here," Mae added. "We could have it delivered."

Erin laughed.

When the last crumbs were gone, the girls crawled in the shelter where the trunk made a ceiling. Mae slid in behind her under the roots. Their slightest moves were exaggerated by the rustle of the garbage bag beneath them.

Erin lay in the darkness and listened to the river, not more than thirty feet away. She wondered if elephants and mastodons had really roamed the Sierra Nevada like archaeologists said. Their bones were supposedly found by miners washing gold-gravel.

Mae shivered. "Wish I had a heavy jacket."

"...a sleeping bag."

"An iPod."

"Last week's leftovers—cold and stale."

Mae breathed in the cold air and coughed. Erin showed her how to breathe into cupped hands and take in warmer air. She wished they had heavier clothes too. A camp stove, a flashlight. Compass. The list was endless.

"My grandma has a saying," Erin whispered, listening to the fire. "'In the school of woods, there is no graduation day.'"

Mae tossed a jagged rock from the shelter. "What does that mean?"

"No matter how much you learn," Erin said, "there's a bunch you still need to know."

"Your grandmother sounds like a cool lady. But isn't it boring living with her? What do you do without a TV?"

Erin rolled onto her stomach. Gram didn't have air-conditioning. No computer. Not even a cordless phone. Just the one attached to the kitchen wall with a thick black cord. Erin didn't miss having a TV. She passed hours reading and writing songs. Music filled space. She mentally added paper and a pen to her wish list.

Erin remembered the look on Gram's face when she heard computers had buttons so people could throw away mail without reading it. "That's like someone walking out of the room while you're talking to him," Gram had said, wrinkling her forehead.

"No, it's never boring," Erin finally said. She remembered the potted plant Gram had given her when she and her dad moved in. The note with the plant had said, "It doesn't matter where your roots come from. You'll make new roots as you grow."

Mae rolled on her side. "It must have been tough, having your mom leave like that."

Erin didn't answer. I'd like to spend one day without thinking about my mother, she thought. But now that Mae had brought up the subject, the same old questions flooded into Erin's head. Why had Lannie left home so suddenly? Had she really been in a hospital? If she was sick, why didn't she go to their family doctor? None of it made sense.

"Don't feel sorry for me," Erin said.

Mae grew quiet. "I feel sorry for your mom."

Erin looked at her, surprised. "I don't want to talk about Lannie, okay?" she said. "I don't want to *think* about her."

"Okay," Mae said softly.

The moon peeked over the stark mountaintops. Its face was startling, as if it was spying on them. Both girls jumped every time a pinecone burst in the fire.

Erin hugged herself against the cold, pretending to be asleep. She huddled in her ragged clothes, willing herself to think about anything except Lannie. All she could conjure up were images of food.

Reaching into a bag of marshmallows and pinching off a sugary chunk. Dipping a spoon into a hot fudge sundae. She tried to switch onto another subject, but had no luck. Erin bit off a hangnail, mad at herself because her thoughts always returned to Lannie.

Sometime in the middle of the night, Erin's stomach protested all the iodine water and greasy chips. She rolled from the shelter, swayed to her feet, and threw up in the bushes. She grabbed a root with one hand and wiped her mouth with the other. Her legs felt like jelly. Her skin burned. She hoped she didn't have a fever.

Then the shivers set in. Her body shook uncontrollably for a few seconds. Unfair. Maybe she hadn't waited long enough after putting iodine in her water bottle before drinking. She squatted behind a tree and peed, thankful she didn't have the runs.

Erin crawled back into the shelter, sweaty and cold. Her stomach still hurt. Her throat was dry. She lay on the hard ground, curled up with her head on her arms, and stared up at the sky.

What if people were like stars? she wondered. Maybe we're so far away from each other all we can see are shadows of who we really are.

The chills eased up, then quit. Erin closed her eyes and fell into a restless sleep.

CHAPTER TEN

*If you pick up a starving dog and make him
prosperous, he will not bite you.*
—MARK TWAIN

Erin awoke again in the night, her stomach rocking
and rolling. Her nose was numb, her fingers stiff
and sore. She felt the hard lumps under the
garbage bag. The fire's earlier light had died to a
flicker. She should add wood, but she was too tired
to get up. Hunger pinched her from the inside.

She listened to the rustling wind and Mae's light
snoring. Even with Mae next to her she felt alone.
*Mae's cluelessness out here makes it seem like I
know more than I do,* she thought wearily.

Suddenly a series of barks and yelps sliced
through the silence of the canyon.

Mae bolted awake. "What's that?"

"Coyotes." Erin peered out. "Sounds like a pack."

"What?"

"Don't worry," Erin put in quickly. "Coyotes don't
attack people." She shivered, blew on her fingers,
and crawled out of the shelter. "I'll put more wood
on the fire."

Just in case, she said to herself.

Erin moved slowly in the dark. She watched, waited. Nothing moved. "Add flashlight to our wish list," she whispered to Mae.

Mae looked out. "Maybe it's...bears?"

"Bears don't bark. And anyway, they're only a problem where there's food."

"Well, aren't we lucky."

Another yelp cut the night air. Mae groaned and quickly drew inside.

Erin felt as weak as watered-down soup. The campsite began to spin. Don't faint, she warned herself, dragging a limb to the fire. You can't collapse now.

She barely made it back to the shelter before falling to her knees. She lay in a heap of shivers and tried to sleep. Her mind wouldn't settle down. She wondered how Indians carried live embers from one camp to another. Probably in clay pots. Gram would know. She'd know what to do about intestinal problems too. She'd be able to name several wild herbs that could calm an upset stomach.

On their camping trips, loaded with food and gear, Erin had always felt that the mountains were welcoming. She had never thought of the Sierra Nevada as possible killers. Now they seemed full of danger.

She rolled over, finally allowing drowsiness to fill her, and dreamed of Gram's camp bread baking in a

Dutch oven buried in white-hot coals. When she woke up it was closer to dawn. A cold wind blew through the woods, shaking the trees and causing rain to spray from pine needles. Then the air was still. Branches overhead made a rasping sound. Twigs broke. A pause. The scratching began again, moving closer to the shelter.

"Coyotes?" Mae whispered harshly.

Erin listened. "Raccoons forage along rivers. Maybe we moved into a den."

"They're vegetarians, right?" Mae sounded scared.

"They eat apples from Gram's tree," Erin said. She didn't tell her that a raccoon had also broken into Gram's chicken coop and made a meal of a prized hen.

Erin couldn't remember if she'd seen scat near the hollow. Not that she knew what raccoon droppings actually looked like.

An owl hooted, *Whoo, hoo-hoo, whoo, whoo.* Gram called owls "the night watchmen of the gardens." She knew the difference between the hoots of a barn owl, an elf owl, and a great horned owl. To Erin they all sounded the same.

Another twig snapped just outside of the shelter. The scratching grew louder.

"I'd rather die of starvation than be mauled by a wild animal," Mae muttered.

Erin's pulse moved from a walk to a jog. She was

ready to run, but there wasn't a back way out of the shelter.

"Somebody's out there," Mae whispered.

Erin peered out between the roots of the sheltering tree at the tangled branches, stark against the early morning sky. She didn't see anything. No bears. No deer. No coyotes. No raccoons. "Maybe it's just the wind."

Another branch cracked.

The girls strained to listen.

Suddenly something large and furry burst into the shelter. Mae screamed, wrestling past Erin to get out. Erin scrambled out behind her.

In the predawn shadows a mud-caked dog barked at them and wagged his tail.

"Oh, wow, I don't believe it!" Mae pulled the cowboy's collie into a hug. "Sequoia!"

CHAPTER ELEVEN

*I ran away twice; once at about 13,
and once at 17. There is not much satisfaction in it,
even as a recollection.*
—MARK TWAIN

Frin and Mae huddled by the fire with Sequoia, watching the sky lighten, happy to have some company. Dawn and dusk were normally Erin's favorite times. One thing fades and something new takes its place, she thought. Someday she'd write a song about it. She'd call it "Metamorphosis."

Morning hurled an amber glow down the mountain, over the boulders, across the river. Erin spread out the map on her lap, holding the pieces together where it was torn. Mae used her brush to pull burrs from Sequoia's matted fur. His ribs stuck out, bony as the ridges surrounding their camp.

"He's starving," Erin said, ignoring the rumbles in her own stomach.

"What about Jake?" Mae untangled a twig from Sequoia's tail. "The poor guy."

"He's probably in the hospital—eating a big stack of pancakes and fat sausages."

Mae didn't believe her, Erin could tell. She picked a blade of grass, chewing absently, and studied the river where it snaked around a sharp bend. "Fish," she said.

"We don't have a pole," Mae pointed out. "What're we going to do? Sweep our T-shirts through the water and hope to snag one?"

"Indians made traps. Baskets, shaped like a funnel," Erin said. "Fish can swim in, but they can't swim out."

"Think we can make one?"

Erin looked around. "We need something to tie the twigs together."

"Would dental floss work?" Mae asked.

"Sure," Erin said. "Do you have some?"

"In my makeup bag."

Erin watched the haze of thin, high clouds billowing in from the west. "It'll take time to make a trap."

"Then we'd better hurry."

The grim urgency in Mae's voice gave Erin new energy. "Okay," she said. "Let's get to work."

A chilling wind whipped dead leaves into whirlwinds of dust. Erin sat by the river stripping leaves off twigs. She measured one twig against another, singing softly under her breath as she worked. It was the same song that had rattled around in her head yesterday.

Tumble
on down the road,
dusty old desert weed...

The beginnings of a cinquain poem. Two syllables in the first line, four on the next. Five lines in all. Twenty-two syllables total. When Erin had first started composing songs, she wrote in couplets: two rhyming lines, one after the other. None of her song-poems rhymed anymore. She didn't have the patience to search for sounds that copied each other. She'd rather think about words for their meaning.

Erin glanced nervously at the gray clouds rolling in over the trees as Mae tied the last twig in place.

"Check the knots," Erin told her. "Make sure they're solid."

Mae cut the floss with a pair of nail clippers. She turned the funnel-shaped trap over in her hands. "What'll keep the fish from swimming out?"

"Guess we need to weave another basket." Erin sighed.

"Pass the twigs," Mae said.

The morning had turned hot and sticky. A faint breeze stirred the air and died. In the stillness it seemed as if the valley was holding its breath. The only things moving were the girls' fingers on the basket-like trap.

Finally Erin set it in the shallow water, pushing the twig box over the narrow end of the funnel. She anchored the trap with rocks.

"Now we wait," she said.

"Think it'll work?" Mae asked hopefully.

"It has to or—" Erin didn't finish.

They had already stopped brushing dried leaves off their clothes and pulling stickers from their socks. They'd even stopped talking about the search-and-rescue team. Mae didn't mention Levi much anymore. Right now they just had to find a way to survive.

Mae gathered their muddy clothes and scrubbed them in the river. Erin walked downstream past storm-beaten trees, amazed at all the wildflowers taking root in the rocky soil. She recognized a plant in the carrot family by its white flowers and fernlike leaves. She knew that Indians ate the boiled roots of certain wild carrots. Her hand brushed the feathery plant, but she didn't dig it up. Poison hemlock was in the same family as wild carrot.

Erin had heard about kids in Lone Pine who had been poisoned after blowing on whistles made from the plant's hollow stems. She made a mental note to study her grandma's book on edible plants.

A quick search for berries or wild fruits produced no results. Erin made a pouch with the hem of her shirt and gathered some miner's lettuce and wild clover, plants she knew were safe to eat.

When she got back to their camp, she dumped the greens on a flat rock. "Salad?"

Mae made a face. "What? No dressing?"

Erin sat on a log and gagged down a mouthful of the bitter greens, hoping they wouldn't come back up. "Indians ate the larvae of ants, wasps, and other insects," she told Mae.

Mae nibbled a leaf. "Don't even think about it."

Erin waded into the stream to inspect the trap. Water rippled clear through the twigs: No fish. Curious, Sequoia followed her. He nosed around the shallow pools, then stood on the bank, shaking himself off. Mae took the bandannas to him and retied them around his neck. She spotted something yellow on the ground behind a large boulder. It was the piece of yellow plastic Jake had made into a rain poncho.

"Look at this," Mae said, picking it up. "Do you think it's the yellow thing we saw yesterday?"

"Maybe." Erin tried not to show her disappointment.

"I wanted it to be a pack," Mae said. "Something human."

"Hey, who gets what they want all the time?" Erin asked.

"Not me, that's for sure," Mae answered.

"I'm way ahead of you," Erin said. "You'll have to take a ticket and get in line."

"Is that another one of your grandmother's sayings?"

Erin sat on a log. "I don't remember. I heard it somewhere."

Mae moved behind her and started separating Erin's tangled hair. "So you were running away, huh?"

Erin stiffened. She almost denied it. But she knew that would be a lie.

"Hey, who am I going to tell?" Mae prodded her.

Erin closed her eyes while Mae's fingers worked. She had been running away, in a sense. Running away from Lannie, anyway.

"Well, I don't blame you," Mae kept on. "Not after your mom was gone a whole year. Did she call at least?"

Erin wished she had earplugs.

"Your grandmother would've told you if she did. Right?"

"Yeah. Gram acted surprised to hear from her," Erin said, on a long sigh. She hadn't realized she'd been holding her breath.

She sat as rigid as the log, picking at a bug bite on her arm. Until now, she hadn't considered how one careless decision could lead to so many others. She looked back on all the stupid things she'd done over the last few days. Losing the bus ticket. Hitchhiking. Now, hiking without being fully prepared.

I should've looked ahead, Erin told herself in a big pulse of sadness. Gram will be so disappointed in me.

Erin wondered if her grandma was home from Bodie by now. If not today, tomorrow for sure. Would a message be waiting on the answering machine? "Erin wasn't on the bus," Lannie would blurt in uncontrolled hysteria. "I've never been so frightened in my whole life!"

Erin stared at the river where it disappeared

around a wide bend. Maybe her mother didn't care that she hadn't showed up.

It made more sense to imagine no messages.

Just like the last eleven months.

CHAPTER TWELVE

Kites rise highest against the wind—not with it.
— Sir Winston Churchill

E rin waded into the river to check the fish trap. "I think we caught something," she told Mae, lifting the box. Water slopped over the sides. A rainbow shimmered between the twigs. Tiny black splotches peppered the scales. "Trout."

"Mmm, pan-fried," Mae said. "With ketchup."

Sequoia whined.

Erin tried to be careful, but overbalanced and nearly toppled in the river. She worked her way slowly to the bank. One of the trap's twig boxes shifted off the other as she trudged through the soft sand. More water slopped out. She kept her eyes on the trap to make sure the fish was still there, hardly believing they'd caught something. She didn't care if it wasn't the legal size. It was...*breakfast.*

Sequoia jumped up to see for himself. "No!" Erin shouted at him. "Down!" He barked and jumped again, knocking the trap from her hands.

"Oh, no!" Mae cried. "Sequoia!"

Erin stood barefoot in the icy water, watching the smallest trout she'd ever seen swim away. "If we didn't have bad luck we wouldn't have any luck at all," she said, her feet aching with cold.

"He didn't mean it," Mae said with a sigh.

Erin was so upset she had trouble reassembling the trap. Her T-shirt felt as if it was melting to her skin. Then the wind shifted and clouds cast shadows over their camp.

Sequoia turned, his nose thrust forward, his tail and ears flattened. Suddenly he began to bark, running in a circle. Then he bolted up the canyon.

"Sequoia!" Mae hollered, running after him. She tripped on a rock and fell.

Erin rushed over. "Are you okay?"

Mae shook her off. "I'm fine. I thought when people were lost, they sent out helicopters, tracked with bloodhounds, sounded sirens. Why isn't anyone looking for us?"

"Rangers would have formed a search party as soon as they found out we were missing," Erin told her. She wondered if Gram would join the searchers when she got home. No, she'd probably stay by the phone and field calls.

"So where are they?" Mae demanded. She dabbed spit on her knee where she'd scraped it. The skin was already puffy and plum colored. "I can't spend another night out here! And now Sequoia's gone."

"He'll come back."

"Sequoia!" Mae yelled.

Erin tried to think of something to make them both feel better. She snatched a garbage bag from the shelter, tied off the holes with floss, and filled the bag with river water. Then she climbed on a boulder and tied the bag to a limb. She figured it would take about an hour for the sun to heat the water. "Hot shower?" Erin said cheerfully.

Mae forced a smile.

Erin knew they were okay again—at least for now.

Time crept by while they watched the trap. One trout wouldn't make a meal for two people. They had to catch four or five fish.

"So what do rangers do out here?" Mae said.

"Help people...or try to. Enforce rules." Erin put on her dirty socks and sneakers and cleaned her knife, ready to gut any fish they caught. "Fix trails. Pack out trash."

"Pack it in, pack it out," Mae said. "Even I know that rule."

All of a sudden, Sequoia burst from the brush on the far side of the river. He raced along the bank as if he couldn't figure out how he'd wound up over there.

"What's that in his mouth?" Mae said.

Erin saw it too. The object was brown, the size of a football. "I don't know."

The dog leaped onto a rotting tree that reached partway across the river, deadwood blown over in a storm. The butt-end of the trunk had fallen in a swirl of rapids. He crept across the tree, then jumped in the shallow water and splashed the rest of the way to the bank.

"A hiking boot," Erin muttered when Sequoia dropped his prize at their feet. The boot wasn't muddy like something left out in a storm. It wasn't old either, just broken in.

"Looks like blood on the heel," she said, frowning.

"Blood? Do you think—" Mae glanced up the canyon.

Erin knew what she was thinking. "The missing ranger?"

Sequoia jumped back in the water, dog-paddled to the downed tree, and clawed his way up to the opposite bank. "He wants us to follow him," Mae said.

"We should stay here near our camp," Erin protested. "And anyway, it would be too hard to get across the river."

"But what if Sequoia found someone? We can't just sit here and wonder. There's bound to be a place where we can get across."

"If we had a rope we could rig a hand line," Erin said, "and tie one end to a tree on this side of the river. That way we could steady ourselves while we cross it."

"I know how to swim," Mae said.

"That's not the point. The water's too fast for us to swim across, and the rocks are too slippery for us to wade."

Erin threw a twig into the river. Then she sat on her heels, studying the current. The twig bounced over boulders where the water boiled white, shot into the air, and snagged on a tangle of roots.

The stretch of water below the point where a person crossed should be long and shallow, she knew. Three people were better than two when crossing without a rope. Three people could form a stable triangle, with the downstream person facing upstream.

Erin grabbed her shoes and socks. "Put your sneakers back on," she told Mae, hoping the shoes had enough rubber left to protect their feet. "And we need strong sticks," she said. "Three or four feet long. To use as a third leg."

While Mae tested sticks, Erin took up her pack. Luckily, the bank wasn't too steep. It was shallow enough where they had anchored the fish trap.

"We have to link arms," Erin said. She tied the boot to her belt loops and stepped into the water. "You face downstream, I'll face up."

Mae stared at her. "You want me to go backwards?"

Their gazes crossed like lances.

"I didn't mean *walk* backwards," Erin snapped. "We'll step sideways. But it'll be steadier if we aren't both facing the same way."

"Don't you just ever just *do* stuff?" Mae asked, shaking her head.

Erin shrugged. "Swim if you want."

Mae muttered under her breath, turned downstream, and hooked her arm through Erin's out-stretched elbow. Erin bent her arm and braced her fist against her own bony hip, tightening their link. Each time before taking a step, she used her stick to check the depth of the water. Every probe took time and demanded careful attention. Their moves were slow and awkward.

At the halfway mark, Erin stumbled. She clutched her stick tighter, wondering if there was a safer way across. The river seemed everywhere, ripping and pulling at them. It seemed wider now that they were thigh-deep. The shore seemed further away, the sand softer, less stable. The icy water stung their legs.

"I forgot to take my watch off," said Mae. "It's not waterproof." She took a step too quickly, throwing both of them off balance.

"Don't lift your feet!" Erin shouted over her shoulder. "You'll slip on a rock."

"How am I supposed to walk if I can't lift my feet?"

Mae was trying to be difficult. As if she needed to try.

"Shuffle," Erin said. Rocks could be stepping-stones. They could also be their slippery ruin.

Slowly, the girls reached the rapids, rolling and tumbling loud as thunder. The bubbling water hadn't looked quite so treacherous from the bank. But near the rocks the current was fighting mad, a crushing surge. Erin used all her strength to fight back.

A shock of wind slammed down the canyon and punched her in the face.

The river doesn't want us here, Erin thought wearily. It wants to take us down. Cut us off. Close us in.

She leaned into the gusts, her top-heavy pack throwing her off-balance. Her sneakers were frozen to her feet. She couldn't feel her toes at all, just her legs being stabbed by invisible icicles. If she stepped on something slippery or sharp she'd never know it.

Erin felt a violent jerk. She dug her stick in the sand, struggling to shift her weight, her muscles practically inside out with cold. She turned in the swift, thigh-high water, lurching against the raging foam.

Mae pulled her arm away, trying to regain her balance. Frantic, she slipped again and let out a sharp cry.

Then she went under.

CHAPTER THIRTEEN

True friendship isn't about being there when it's convenient; it's about being there when it's not.
—ANONYMOUS

Mae wasn't exactly swimming. She was flailing to keep from going under again, her mud-streaked face scrubbed by the river's boiling course. Erin jammed her weight against the stick, reaching toward Mae with her free hand. She felt new strength, determination. "Grab on!"

Mae sputtered and took hold.

They still had twenty feet left to go to the far shore. The current had grown stronger, much stronger. White water pounded them, almost blinding them with foamy spray. I hope there aren't any deep holes nearby, Erin thought with a sudden shock. She poked ahead with her stick and took a small step.

"Don't let go!" she yelled, though she hated to waste the breath.

Over the roar of the rapids she heard Mae cry, "I'm not gonna make it!"

She's right. This is impossible, Erin thought, feeling herself being dragged down by the extra weight. But she kept going, probing with the hand holding the stick, pulling Mae with the other. One step, then another. "We're almost there!" she yelled.

Erin staggered on. She didn't let go of Mae for a second.

The two of them struggled out of the water, then dropped to the ground. They lay still for a few moments, letting the warmth of sun-baked rocks seep up through their wet clothes.

Sequoia ran circles around them, barking. It was as if he were saying, *What took you so long?*

* * *

Another hot day. Hotter and longer than the day before.

Yesterday Erin and Mae had hiked into the valley by way of the west-facing slope.

Now they were following Sequoia up the side of the mountain that rose abruptly from the river. The ground was choked with scratchy brush. They walked and climbed with the hazy sun beating down on them. The midday rays were intense. Sweat poured off their bodies, but their clothes dried quickly.

From time to time the dog doubled back and checked on them, then ran ahead again.

We should have been leaving clues for a search

party, breaking branches along the way, Erin thought suddenly. I could have used my knife to scratch marks in trees. She nearly laughed. At least Hansel and Gretel had the sense to leave bread crumbs, even if birds did eat them.

Erin thought about how little she and Mae had eaten in the last two days—and she'd lost most of what was in her stomach in the bushes. How were they staying on their feet? She had no idea.

She looked down the canyon at the river shimmering below. They had spread the yellow slicker on a boulder and secured it with river stones, making the camp easier to spot from a distance. She was surprised they'd covered so much ground so quickly.

In her mind, she heard Gram say, *You can go more than a week without food if you have water.*

Erin took a tug on her water bottle. No matter what Gram said, there was no way they could keep up this pace for a week without food. Hike. Sweat. Rest. Fill up on water.

The fear of stopping and not being able to get started again kept Erin's legs pumping. You can do this, she told herself. Just keep going…

With each step Erin's mind marched over their problems: food, shelter, how much trail they would cover each day. Step, step, step. The granite under foot made her body ache. Every one of her muscles seemed stretched to the breaking point.

If we hike long enough, she wondered, wouldn't there be a point where our fatigue would vanish?

Sort of like being in a trance? Maybe we'd be aware of pain but it'd no longer consume us. *Endorphins.* That was the name of the body's natural painkiller.

Erin glanced at Mae, wondering how she managed to keep up. Mae was definitely tougher than she acted.

The girls hiked on, crawling over fallen trees and clambering over outcrops of granite. The sun-beaten slopes grew steeper, the underbrush thinner. Their arms and legs were a maze of scratches. Every step was as hot and dusty as the last. The tall grass told Erin no one had traveled this way in a long time. They hadn't seen Sequoia for at least half an hour.

They passed a grove of charred trees, the upper limbs blasted off by lightning. Erin shivered. The fallen trees had a deathlike calm. The needles were still green.

Not far beyond the blackened trees, they spotted Sequoia standing stone still in an open spot.

"He's watching something," Erin said. "Hunting, maybe."

"Hope he'll share," Mae muttered.

"You want to skin a poor animal with fur?" Erin asked.

"No thanks," Mae said quickly.

Erin curved around a colony of lily-like plants. She barely noticed the beautiful clusters of stark flowers. Is any part of a lily safe to eat? she wondered. White flowers? Stem? Root?

She remembered the poison hemlock and kept moving. Weeds tickled her legs. A cloud of gnats parted to let her pass. She started humming the song she'd been working on. "Tumble on down the road," she sang softly, "dusty old desert weed…"

"Garth Brooks?" Mae asked.

Erin would rather have been compared to throaty Melissa Etheridge. "It's one of mine," she said.

"Huh. Ever sing in a band?"

"I sing in church, if that counts," Erin said.

"Sure, I count it," Mae said.

Sequoia stopped again, sniffing the ground where two slabs of granite jutted out from the side of the mountain. Between the slabs, an opening the width of a tree trunk split the center. Sequoia barked and vanished inside.

"A cave," Erin said.

Mae peered in the opening. "I can't see anything."

"Look for a pine limb green enough to have sap," Erin said.

Mae found one.

Erin took the film canister from her pocket and struck a match, holding it to the re-lighting birthday candle. The match blew out before the candle caught. "Crap!" she muttered. "We can't afford to waste any matches."

She slouched against the wind and struck a second match. The candle caught, barely. Just when it looked as if the wind had blown out the flame again, the wick flared up. She used the candle to light the pine branch torch.

"Come on," she said.

Mae hung back. "I can't. I'm claustrophobic."

Erin shot her a look, shaking her head. Then she squeezed inside.

"Wait up!" Mae called. Erin held the torch in front of her. Mae stood so close Erin could hear her breathe. Burning sap and pine needles tempered the darkness with fragile light. Shadows danced on the walls; flecks of quartz sparkled in the torch-light.

Erin took a deep breath. "Hello?"

Her voice bounced back. *Lo...lo...lo.*

Erin ran her free hand along the rough stone and inched forward. She coaxed Mae along a few feet at a time. Sometimes the ceiling dropped and they had to duck. The floor was hard-packed with bony ridges that caught the toes of their sneakers.

Something skittered overhead, stirring up the stink of bird poop. It smelled like there were mounds of it. "What was that?" Mae whispered.

"Bats."

Mae groaned.

Erin called out again. "Anybody there?"

There...there... The word echoed back.

"Do snakes like caves?" Mae whispered.

"Sequoia would've scared them off," Erin said.

"You sure?"

Erin heard in Mae's voice how much she wanted to believe her. "Yeah."

Another bend and the tunnel opened up to a dimly lit chamber. Light the color of the late afternoon filtered down through an opening at the top of the cave. A swirl of wind blew through the hole: Nature's air conditioning. Against the wall, on the far side of the burnished circle, several roundish lumps lay in the shadows. The lumps seemed planned, in some sort of order.

Erin moved closer, torch in hand. The flame flickered in the downdraft.

The lumps came into focus: A large backpack and rolled sleeping bag.

Sequoia barked. He nudged the pack. Erin took another step and froze. One lump was a person. Trembling, she held out the torch. When the wind nearly blew it out, she drew it back.

The man was lying on a rain slicker. His eyes were closed, like he was sleeping. Wavering shadows gave him a spooky appearance.

"Mister?" Erin said. "Hello?"

No answer.

Erin took another step. "Are you okay?"

The man wore a gray shirt with a brown patch labeled National Park Service. Forest green shorts. Missing boot. One foot twisted backwards.

Mae moved closer. "Is he unconscious?" she asked.

Erin was in a daze, unable to speak. It occurred to her that the ranger's last thoughts must have been of his family back in Ridgecrest. Those poor little boys. She knew how sad they'd be when they heard the news.

Mae covered her eyes. "God! He's dead!" A second later her last word echoed from the rock walls.

Dead...dead...dead...

CHAPTER FOURTEEN

You have to endure what you can't change.
—MARIE DE FRANCE

Fear swirled in the dank cave, wrapping itself around the girls. Erin forced herself to answer. "Yeah. He's...dead." Her voice seemed everywhere at once, an ear-piercing throb. *Dead! Dead! Dead!* She felt like she was going crazy.

Mae began to sob quietly. She knelt beside Sequoia, wrapped her arms around his neck, and drew him closer. Mae buried her face in the collie's fur. Her muffled scream reverberated in the cold empty space.

Sequoia squirmed free, his tail swiping the air. He trotted over to the ranger's backpack and nudged it with his nose. A flashlight and ball cap lay on top.

Erin set her pack on the ground and moved toward the ranger.

"No! You can't touch him," Mae muttered.

As if in answer, a howl of wind from the hole in the ceiling snuffed the torch. Erin shuddered and forced herself to pick up first the flashlight, then the ranger's pack. Her muscles protested under the weight. Her shoulders didn't seem broad enough, strong enough.

"We can't take his stuff," Mae said in a small voice. "It...it isn't right."

"We don't have any choice. He might have food."

Food...Food, echoed the walls. Mae sighed. "Shouldn't we say a few words?" she asked quietly.

Erin thought about the dozens of songs she'd written. Snatches of ballads. Folk songs. Nothing seemed quite right. Then she remembered a poem she'd memorized at her new school. She started to recite the lines slowly. *"I sing to use the waiting, my bonnet but to tie..."* She stumbled over the middle lines, but the last two came to her clearly. *"And tell each other how we sang to keep the dark away."*

Mae hefted Erin's pack. "Perfect."

"Emily Dickinson," Erin said. "It's called 'Waiting'."

The beam from the ranger's flashlight bounced with Erin's steps, sweeping the floor of the cave in wide arcs. Once she stumbled and the unwieldy pack threw her against the wall.

"You okay?" asked Mae.

"I'm all right," Erin answered. But she wasn't all right. She was hungry, tired, cold.

"Where's the entrance to the tunnel?" Mae asked.

"Over there," said Erin, pointing the way with the flashlight. She walked into a spider web and brushed it from her face. She felt like crying. They didn't even know the ranger's name. She realized he probably had a wallet in his pocket and other personal belongings. But there was no way she could have looked for them. No way she could have touched him.

When they reached the chamber at the end of the tunnel Erin could smell the bats again.

Mae coughed.

The sound echoed, a jackhammer.

"There isn't enough air in here," she said.

Erin knew Mae was right. She felt like she was strangling. "We're almost out." She tried to sound more positive than she felt.

"Thank god for that flashlight," Mae said with a shiver.

Erin touched the cold rock, flashing the light into a side tunnel. Water trickled down a wall, pooling on the ground.

"I didn't hear any water before." Mae sounded terrified.

Erin listened to the dripping sound. "The entrance is just ahead," she said.

"How come you're always so sure of everything?" Mae said.

"I haven't been sure of anything in a long time," Erin answered.

"Where's Sequoia?" Mae asked.

"He'll catch up," said Erin. "Let's rest just a minute." She leaned against the wall, letting it take some of the weight off her pack. For a moment, her back and shoulders relaxed a bit. If only she could unload other burdens so easily. She remembered Lannie sitting at her computer, hands flying over the keyboard. "I've started a consulting business," she'd said. "I'm going to make so much money you can have anything you want. Just name it, honey."

Up till then Lannie had been a full-time volunteer at Erin's school, shelving books in the library and organizing fundraisers. After school, she'd shuttled Erin and her friends to softball or soccer practice, depending on the season. Lannie always packed healthy snacks and let the girls play their favorite CDs.

Things changed when Lannie started her business. She ate bowls of cereal on the run. Breakfast, lunch, and dinner. She rarely slept. Expensive gifts appeared in Erin's bedroom. Gold boxes with pink ribbon. Silk dresses, beaded, with price tags that showed a small fortune. Did her mom really expect Erin to wear clothes like that? Erin had been confused and bewildered. It was as if some alien had taken over Lannie's body.

Her dad kept asking where the money came from. At first Lannie just smiled, not answering. Then she began striking a pose: arms outstretched, hands grasping his shoulders. "I have infinite resources," she'd said with a confident smile. "Keep the faith."

A few weeks later, Lannie bought a cell phone for

every room in the house, even their two bathrooms. Truckloads of furniture arrived. A brand new SUV, which Erin's dad had promptly returned to the dealer. A sports car took its place.

Then, Lannie's good mood seemed to change all at once, like someone had flipped a switch. A pathetic image rose in Erin's mind: Lannie soaking in the bathtub for hours, using up all the hot water. Her hair stringy as pumpkin guts, clinging to the earphones of her CD player. Her eyes closed, listening to the same songs over and over.

The picture was so real, so strong, Erin could almost smell bubble bath and the scented candles that burned around the tub. She hadn't been able to understand what was going on with Lannie, but she had known this much—something was terribly wrong.

Sequoia barked, jolting Erin back to the cave.

CHAPTER FIFTEEN

*"I think," said Christopher Robin, "that we ought
to eat all our provisions now, so that we shan't
have so much to carry."*
—A. A. MILNE

Erin and Mae staggered behind Sequoia through the narrow opening. Outside, the girls collapsed in the sun. They both gulped fresh air as if they'd been swimming underwater. Mae pretended to kiss the ground. "I didn't think we'd ever get out of there," she said.

Sequoia ran between them, wagging his tail and licking their faces.

"What're we gonna do about...you know..." Mae's voice fell away.

"Rangers will hike in." Erin let the pack slip from her shoulders. "And take him home to be buried."

"I can't believe he's dead," Mae said.

Erin couldn't believe it, either. She'd thought that he might be hurt, but it had never occurred to her that he wasn't alive.

Mae got up and gathered pine branches, marking the cave's opening with a temporary cross. Then she used her lipstick to rub a red heart on the rock. "In case the branches blow over," she said sadly.

"I'm sure he would have appreciated it," Erin told her. She began digging through the ranger's pack. "A bag of dehydrated apples. Peanut butter."

They tore hungrily into the apples. Erin wondered if stomachs could really shrink, like people said. It sure seemed like it. After only a few bites she felt full.

"Can dried fruit go bad?" Mae asked.

"It should be good for months," Erin said. "Besides, the cave is cool, dark, dry."

Mae turned toward the cross, ashen-faced. "Thanks."

Erin nodded, knowing the ranger would want them to have his food. She grabbed his pack and squinted up the slope. "It's getting dark."

She and Mae turned their backs on the cave and the ranger and threaded their way down the slope, following the path of an avalanche where no new trees had dared to take root. Erin groaned beneath the ranger's heavy pack. It had to weigh at least forty pounds. Her steps were small, unstable. She shifted the straps to keep them from slicing her shoulders and focused on the lightning-charred trees she'd intentionally memorized on the way up.

"I saw the ranger's ankle," Mae said. "Do you think that killed him?"

"I guess that's what kept him from hiking out. And he was probably exhausted. Dehydrated." Erin paused to catch her breath. "Who knows what else."

"He used the cave for shelter," Mae said.

Erin plodded on. "Yep, looks like it."

She used her hands, tearing her already-ragged nails, to steady herself in a gully that ran between two steep slopes covered with loose rock. No air stirred. "I bet the dirt on my body is old enough to have geological significance," Erin said.

"These mountains wouldn't be so bad if we weren't lost," Mae said.

Erin forced a smile. "And backpacking wouldn't be so bad if the packs were empty."

They reached the valley before the sun dropped behind the mountain peaks. Trudging back and forth along the riverbank, Erin found an easier way to cross the raging water. Exhausted, she and Mae finally stumbled into camp. Sequoia curled up under a tree.

Erin unrolled the ranger's sleeping bag. She and Mae unloaded his pack onto the bag. Erin took inventory: water pump, headlamp, butane lighter, metal bowl, spoon. A thin book by John Muir. A pencil, broken. First-aid kit: adhesive tape, salve, scissors, moleskin. She glanced up at the garbage bag tied to the tree. All the water had leaked out. No hot shower today.

Mae found two pairs of wool socks. She shook out a shirt. The brown patch on the sleeve said National Park Service. Embroidered inside the emblem were a sequoia tree, some mountain peaks, and a bison.

"Shovel," Erin said, unsnapping the handle. "We can dig a cat-hole."

"A what?"

"A toilet."

Mae made a face, then asked, "Does he have a mirror?"

"No."

"That's good."

Erin stared at Mae. The girl was thinner than when they'd first started. Her face looked longer, but it wasn't really. Just sunken in. Erin was sure they'd each lost seven or eight pounds. That was a lot in three days.

She tried to think of something nice to say. "I like your hair without the purple."

"Mom won't let me dye it for real," Mae said. "I hope she isn't too worried about me," she added wistfully.

Erin gave her a sympathetic smile. Then she pulled a plastic cylinder from the pack. "A bear-proof food canister," she said and tossed Mae a small bag of nuts and chocolate. "Protein!"

"Fat!" Mae dug in. "Sugar!"

Erin sliced chunks of mold off the cheese before making cracker sandwiches. Then she explained to Mae how they would need to ration the rest of the food. "We should save more than we eat," she said. That was the goal, at least. "For the hike out."

"Can we can make it in one day?" Mae asked.

Erin glanced at the silky wisps of clouds over-head. "Maybe. With the ranger's food and clothes we have the hiker's three Ws: water, warmth, and wool."

She pulled a topography map out of its plastic holder and unfolded it. "I see where we messed up," she said, trailing a finger over a squiggly brown line. "How we got so far off track."

"We've always had a map," Mae said, frowning.

"Not as good as this one."

Mae offered Sequoia a bit of cheese. He snatched it from her hungrily, nearly nipping one of her fingers. "That's all for now," she said to the dog. "You're on rations too."

Mae took the map from Erin and marked the route to the cave with the pencil. "So we'll remember the way."

"Good idea," Erin said. She put twigs on the fire. Smaller pieces of wood would burn to ash quicker and be easier to clean up in the morning. The fire cracked and spit. Its light made a small circle of warmth.

Yeah, Erin told herself. Maybe they could hike out in one day. Tomorrow.

She gathered the sun-baked clothes she had left on the rocks earlier and shook out their stiffness. She left the yellow slicker where it was on the slim chance that a search party might see it.

Although the sky had begun to darken, there was

still a glow of light on the canyon's western slope. Small pools of rain shimmered everywhere: on ridges and in piles of stones pushed aside by ancient glaciers. When the sun finally set, an awful stillness hushed everything in the landscape.

The girls worked together by the firelight. Mae put a handful of dehydrated apples in the metal bowl and covered it with water. "It'll be softer in the morning," she said. "Fruit for breakfast."

Erin dug deeper in the backpack and pulled out a bag of light-colored grain. "Couscous."

Mae made a face. "Sounds gross."

"It's crushed pasta," Erin said. She opened the packet and poured water over the coarse particles. "Lunch."

They crept under the shelter and settled in, spreading the ranger's sleeping bag over them. It felt good, almost as if it was protecting them.

Mae hugged Sequoia. "You stink, boy."

"Not as bad as I do," Erin said.

"No kidding." Mae giggled.

Erin laughed, too.

They listened to the night wind blowing off the higher peaks. After a while it gained strength, moaning through the canyons. Erin turned on her side, watching the fire struggle. Wind scattered sparks. Every time she closed her eyes she saw the ranger and thought about his two little boys. She stared at the glowing embers of their campfire, sure the night would never end.

Erin wondered if Gram had called her dad in South America. But surely she'd talked with Lannie first. When Gram heard Erin never showed up, she'd probably be on the phone with every bus station from Bishop to Camarillo. Would the clerk in Big Pine remember her? Not very likely.

Gram wouldn't hesitate to call her friends at the sheriff's station in Lee Vining. She had probably taken them a snapshot of Erin too.

She rolled on her side and nestled under the warm sleeping bag. Dark whispered through the trees.

CHAPTER SIXTEEN

Strangers are just friends waiting to happen.
— UNKNOWN

Erin awoke in the night. A chilly dew beaded the sleeping bag. She thought she'd heard something, but she wasn't sure. She lifted her head and scanned the dark shelter. *Nothing.* She lay down and listened again.

You've been dreaming, Erin told herself. Go back to sleep.

She huddled under the sleeping bag and adjusted the rolled sweatshirt she was using for a pillow. She heard roots scraping the garbage bag overhead. Beside her, Mae's breathing was even. Sequoia whimpered and twitched in his doggie dreams.

Toward morning the shelter was cold and speckled with moonlight. Slowly, the sky began to show the first hint of light. No reason to build up the fire, Erin thought. We'll be on our way soon. She took a swallow from her water bottle and sampled the soggy coucous. Cold couscous for breakfast was the worst thing she'd ever tasted. It was also the most delicious.

She slipped on her shoes and rubbed her hands briskly above the last coals in the fire pit. Her fingers were chapped from exposure, cold, and constant use. She smeared the open cracks with lip balm, hoping they wouldn't start bleeding.

Sequoia nudged his nose under Erin's hand. "Come on, boy," she said, scratching his head. "Let's check the trap."

Thud.

Startled, Erin turned.

A rust-red squirrel worked feverishly in a nearby tree, severing pinecones. She recognized it as a chickaree. Most creatures tried to move quietly in the wilderness. Not squirrels. They constantly chattered and scolded.

"Having breakfast?" she asked.

Sequoia barked and took off after the squirrel.

"Don't go far," she called after him. "We're heading out soon."

Erin dragged the trap from the river. Trout—three of them. "Our luck is changing," she muttered, feeling hopeful.

Low gray clouds smudged the sky. She worked quickly in the cold, gathering river grass. She returned to the fire and covered the last coals with the wet grass. It sizzled and hissed. She dug a small hole in the dirt, then wiped the blade of her knife on her shirt. Taking a deep breath and holding the fish firmly, she slit the belly from the back fin to its head and scraped the guts into the hole. Don't want to attract bears, she thought, kicking dirt over it.

She placed the fish on the steaming grass and covered them with a top layer. She'd never cooked trout before. But sandwiching them between layers of river grass seemed like a good idea. The smell of smoldering fish rose with the smoke from the fire.

The sky paled over the eastern ridges as Erin sat by the burning embers. Mist lay in blotches along the ground. The wet, dark tree trunks looked sleepy in the gloomy light. Drowsiness wrapped itself around her.

It was hard to believe she and Mae had spent three nights in the wilderness. They'd been through so much together. It seemed like eons since she'd met Mae at that store.

The mountains have taught us some serious lessons, Erin thought. She felt years older and she knew Mae probably did too. She stayed a while by the fire, then put on her sweatshirt.

The inky shadows filling the canyon worried her. Wind whistled a warning and clouds spilled over the peaks. Dried leaves spun through space. She shuddered at the unmistakable flash of lightning. Then thunder broke the air wide open.

How many seconds between the thunder and lightning? The next time it flashed she counted to thirty before the thunder rumbled and divided by five, remembering another formula for calculating the distance of storms. Only six miles away. Six miles was nothing out here.

The forest growled as Mae crawled out of the shelter. "What was that?"

Erin hesitated long enough to see lightning snake through the dark sky. Thunder backfired between the rock walls, a clap of doom. Rain blew in from the west. Hail fired at them. Pellets pounded the plastic over the shelter, sounding like a crazed drummer.

Mae looked stunned. "No! Not again!"

Erin pushed her inside and scrambled in behind her. "Guess we won't be hiking today."

"Nature doesn't care about us," Mae said, using a pathetic tone Erin had never heard from her. "We're about as important as a flea bite."

Erin shouted above the din of hail battering the garbage bag. "That doesn't make sense."

"I'm too tired to make sense!" Then Mae shouted, "You weren't so mean at the store."

"And you're just as stupid now as you were then."

"At least my mom didn't ditch me—"

Erin tugged on the sleeping bag and pulled it up to her chin. She huddled beneath the low ceiling, her whole body aching like an open wound.

"Oh, Erin." Mae finally reached over and touched her arm. "I'm so sorry."

Erin shook her hand off.

Mae wouldn't let go. "I don't have any right to say anything about your mother. My mom is so superficial. She only cares about what people think. How things look. That's what matters to her. She volunteers at the homeless shelter to impress her friends. Then she works it into her conversations— how happy those poor people are to get a bowl of soup and hunk of bread."

"At least she's helping other people." Erin snatched a pinecone, rolling it between her hands. The toothy cone-scales scratched her skin. "Lannie doesn't care about anyone but herself."

"And I *hate* the potato pancakes Dad makes on my birthday," Mae reeled on. "He's the one who likes potato pancakes." She sucked in a deep breath, cooling the cogs in her head. "I miss Mom and Dad though. And I'm really sorry, Erin. You know…I didn't mean to say that."

"Forget it." Erin tossed the cone from the shelter. "I'm gonna get my pack." She pushed into the wind-driven rain and spotted Sequoia at the fire pit. She picked up a rock and tossed it at his feet. "Hey! Get away from there!"

Too late. Sequoia had already eaten the trout.

"No more food for you!" Erin shouted at him.

Sequoia hung his head, burnt grass on his whiskers.

Erin crawled back in the shelter and took off her soaked sweatshirt, thankful for the ranger's dry clothes. "Sequoia ate our fish," she said.

Mae shrugged. "If we had bacon we could make bacon and eggs for breakfast."

"If you weren't a vegetarian."

Then they laughed. It was amazing they could laugh at anything.

Erin closed her eyes against the jags of light. She didn't exactly pray, but she went inside her mind for answers. Thunderstorms rarely struck before noon. Why now?

She and Mae stayed quiet, listening to the storm rage around them. Thunder echoed like a distant cannon and swords of lightning slashed the sky.

Erin grabbed a sock and plugged a leak in the ceiling, hammering it in place with her fist. Then a pinhole leak began dripping. She took a shoelace from her sneaker and stuck one end in the hole. She ran the other end into her water bottle, watching the leaking water flow down the string as hail battered the shelter. Finally sunlight slanted through a steady but gentle rain.

Erin emptied the packs onto the sleeping bag, then pushed her smaller day pack inside the ranger's larger backpack. Carefully, she divided up the food: cheese, crackers, peanuts, chocolate.

"There isn't much left," Erin warned. "And it has to last."

"What a way to lose weight," Mae said. She reached into the corner for the bowl of dried apples.

They ate four slices of the softened fruit and put the rest back in the bag.

Erin opened the book she'd found with the ranger's stuff. She used his pencil and scribbled in the margins:

> *Questions*
> *Without answers*

"What're you writing?" Mae asked.

Erin had been thinking about a new song—moving words around in her head, working out the melody. But she wasn't ready to share it.

She flipped to another page in the book. "Listen to this," she said, reading aloud. "'The silvery zigzag lightning lances are longer than usual, and the thunder gloriously impressive, keen, crashing, intensely concentrated, speaking with such tremendous energy it would seem that an entire mountain is being shattered.'"

"The ranger kept a journal?" Mae asked.

"It's *My First Summer in the Sierra* by John Muir," Erin said. "Written more than a hundred years ago."

"That's so cool," Mae said.

"Just think, Muir must've gone through a storm like the one on the ridge."

"And lived to tell about it."

Erin found a newspaper clipping stuck in the book. She noted that it was written by a park ranger in Inyo National Forest. *William Webb.* Could that be *their* ranger?

"'If a thunderstorm threatens, get inside a large building or a car,'" she read aloud from the article. "'Do not stand under a natural lightning rod, such as an isolated tree. Avoid high places and stay away from water.'"

"I know that now," Mae said.

"'If you feel your hair stand on end during a thunderstorm, drop to your knees, bend forward, and—'"

"Kiss your butt good-bye," Mae said.

Erin grinned. "Yeah, that's about it."

She closed the book, tucking the clipping inside.

"You know, sometimes it feels like we're not alone out here," Mae said. "Like there's someone with us."

"The ranger?"

"No. It's like we're being followed." Mae paused as the forest grew quiet. "But not by a real person."

"My grandma talks about that," Erin said. "It's something that happens when you spend a lot of time in the mountains. She says it's ourselves—or the selves we're trying to leave behind."

Mae looked at her strangely. "You mean, like our past?"

"Or some part of it," Erin said.

"So it's kind of like starting over?"

"I guess," Erin answered, wondering if people really could start over.

"Do you believe in ghosts?" Mae asked.

Erin shrugged. "I've never seen one."

The wind blew down the canyon, howling like a hungry coyote.

Erin thought about Lannie.

CHAPTER SEVENTEEN

"Are we going to be friends forever?" asked Piglet.
"Even longer," Pooh answered.
—A. A. MILNE

The rain finally slacked off. When the light drizzle hit the plastic bag ceiling, it sounded like rain on the roof of a car.

Mae pulled a deck of cards from her knapsack. "Poker?"

"What should we play for?" Erin tore off squares of toilet paper. "Who digs the next cat-hole?"

Mae dealt each of them five cards. "Are you saying we're going to be here that long?"

"Okay, then how about this? Loser carries the ranger's pack when we start hiking." Erin wondered if Mae could handle that. Her own shoulders were raw where the straps had dug in.

"You're on." Mae studied her hand of cards. "What did your dad say when your mom left?"

Erin arranged her cards. She threw in three cards and four squares of tissue. "I'm in."

Mae dealt Erin three cards and two for herself. "He had to know where she went, right?"

Erin shifted uncomfortably and tossed in another tissue, even though she only had a pair of fours. It was so weird, the stuff her mom had taken with her: scissors from the kitchen drawer, Dad's alarm clock, her pillow—with the case neatly folded on the bed—and every single one of Dad's framed photos. She'd left behind bent metal hooks and gaping spaces on the walls that screamed, *Something is missing here!*

And then there were the muddy footprints on the carpet, a record of how many trips Lannie had made up and down the stairs to carry stuff out. Why hadn't she taken off her shoes? Or picked a day that wasn't raining?

When her dad saw the muddy mess and missing photos, he knew Lannie had gone. He'd dropped his head so low Erin couldn't see how he could breathe. "Guess she was in a hurry," he'd muttered, like he couldn't think of what else to say.

Rushing to leave, Erin had thought. To leave us.

Erin had listened at the door when her dad called Gram, but she was only able to make out a few words.

Lannie's gone.

We don't know where she went.

Erin didn't understand it. How could she have done this to us?

She felt Mae staring at her. "So didn't you ask him where she went?" Mae asked.

Erin sighed again. "I didn't want to make him feel worse."

"Guess my parents don't seem so bad now," Mae said.

"She didn't tell anyone where she was going," Erin continued. "I don't know why."

Mae just listened as Erin's words tumbled out.

During the first few weeks at Gram's house, she'd marked the days on her calendar until one month had passed, then two. "After awhile Dad started feeling better," Erin said. "At least he acted normal on the outside. He didn't spend hours on the phone anymore, trying to learn something from Lannie's friends."

She glanced over at Mae. "I hate it when kids ask, 'Where's your mom?' Sometimes I say she went out of town on business. Once I said she joined the Peace Corps. When we moved to Lee Vining, I told my new friends she died."

"Too bad we can't pick our parents," Mae said.

Erin threw in her cards. She couldn't talk about this anymore. She felt like she was about to dissolve into nothingness.

This time Mae dealt out all the cards, facedown, in two stacks. "Let's play War."

Erin nodded. War didn't take any brainpower.

Mae scratched Sequoia behind his ears. "Doesn't seem much like summer."

Erin looked out at the low-hanging clouds. No sun. No way to tell the time. Mae's watch had been ruined when they'd crossed the river. "Mountains make their own weather," she said. "Their own seasons even."

They played cards for another couple of hours without bothering to keep track of who won the most games.

Erin crawled out of the shelter, wondering how long it had been since the last rain shower. Most of the clouds had scattered and the sky looked squeaky clean.

Mae climbed out behind her. "Did we lose anything?"

Erin stared at the river. It was swollen and raging over the banks. "The first aid kit," she said, watching the plastic box sink. Their shovel was caught on a snag in the rapids, too far out to reach safely.

"I'll look for the fish trap," Mae said.

Erin tripped on the water filter, half buried in mud. "Good luck."

They eyed the embers in the fire pit. They had been beaten flat by the hail, the ashes washed smooth.

"We should break up the shelter before we go," Erin said.

After striking camp, Erin and Mae took turns going to the bathroom behind a tree stump. They filled their water bottles and studied the route they had marked on the ranger's map. Then, shouldering their packs, they trudged up the rubble-strewn canyon. After about a mile they decided to switch packs. Mae slumped a little under the heavier load, but she didn't complain.

They hiked silently, watching the sun make an arc toward the west. Their path twisted like a dirty string around enormous boulders. It wound toward a gap in a ridge below an area of broken rock buttresses. The trees here seemed to grow from bare rock, clinging to exposed slopes. Stiff winds had sculpted their scrawny branches to one side.

Sequoia kept dashing ahead and disappearing. Then he'd scamper back and lick the girls' hands, begging for a scratch. Erin forgave him for eating the fish. She knew what it felt like to be so hungry her insides seemed hollow.

As the dog darted off again, Erin spotted a small, shrubby pine tree with dense branches. It had dropped its cones, scattering tiny brown seeds on the ground. She crawled on her hands and knees, gathering seeds with dirty fingers, grateful that no animals had beaten them to the treasure. The best thing about pine nuts was that they didn't have to be hulled. "Over here," she called to Mae. "Fill your pockets." She tossed a handful in her mouth, savoring the sweet buttery flavor.

They gathered all the raw nuts they could find, ate about a fourth of them, and put the rest in their packs. Erin didn't feel full. Just…not starving. Gram collected nuts like these and roasted them in the oven. For a special treat she sometimes mixed in homemade candy. Indians had been eating pine nuts for generations.

The girls kept moving.

Erin couldn't find a comfortable rhythm. She watched each step, careful not to split off flakes of granite that might make her lose her footing. They pulled themselves upwards by hanging onto the squatty trees, their shoes sinking ankle-deep in loose shale. For several hundred yards they crept along a dangerously narrow slab of rocky trail, trying not to slip on the shifting surface.

"It's like a rock treadmill, " Mae said.

Erin thought so, too. Sometimes it didn't feel like they were moving ahead at all. She shoved a piece of shale with her sneaker and watched it tumble out of sight. One wrong step and her bones wouldn't be discovered for eons.

Erin and Mae stopped to swap packs. Erin didn't remember the load being so heavy. Every muscle screamed under the strain. The straps dug new trenches in her shoulders. With each step she seemed to be changing the shape of the earth beneath her. Her tattered sneakers, her pack, and the water bottle swinging in her hand all felt like parts of her body.

Erin realized they'd been hiking for hours without a rest. The river and their old camp had disappeared from view. She imagined walking and never stopping. She would simply hike on. A girl with a pack. One foot in front of the other. Leaving her past behind. Hiking to a new day. Someday she'd write a song about it.

If they ever got out of the mountains.

CHAPTER EIGHTEEN

I am not the smartest or most talented person
in the world, but I succeeded because
I keep going and going and going.
— SYLVESTER STALLONE

The trail climbed a steep mass of loose rock lying at the base of a slope, dropped into a boulder-choked ravine, and climbed another slope. The grade was dangerously spiny, littered with shavings of thin rock, weathered and broken off.

Erin slipped, triggering a small landslide.

Mae jumped out of the way, setting off another slide. "Hey, watch it!" She dropped her water bottle and watched in dismay as it bounced down the sheer incline in an avalanche of rock.

"You can share mine," Erin said.

Mae shrugged. "One less thing to carry."

Two-thirds up the incline Erin tripped again, her legs a tangle of fatigue. Any strength she'd had that morning had completely drained out of her body. She pitched sideways. Pain stabbed her shoulders. The ranger's pack shifted, working against her, testing her. One strap slipped.

Let it fall, she thought. Keep walking without it.

No way, another voice said. The map's in there. It will show us the way out.

Erin re-shouldered the strap.

Don't blow it, she told herself.

Every time she stumbled, she thought she'd go down. The drop-off on the boulder side was ten feet on her left. Tripping on an untied shoelace could trigger a landslide. She forced herself to walk closer to the edge, an exercise to stay alert. Half an hour later they slogged through a narrow creek, too tired to jump it. Erin filled the water bottle and dropped in two iodine tablets.

Erin remembered feeling this tired once before.

On the worst days after Lannie left, silence had borne down on the house like a gravestone. Erin had felt wiped out, an emotional exhaustion that went deeper than bone and muscle. She'd slept and slept. Right now that kind of a deep sleep would feel good. Her eyes felt like they were being held open by needles.

The afternoon sun spilled over the rocks like liquid fire. Erin pulled her sticky shirt away from her skin and imagined the cool feel of freshly washed sheets.

The girls finally stopped to rest, sharing more pine nuts and dried fruit.

Mae poured water from Erin's bottle into her cupped hand for Sequoia. The collie greedily lapped it up. He seemed happy enough, even though his ribs stuck out and his fur was muddy.

Erin dropped the pack with a grunt and studied the map. She rotated it, trying to align the forms on the paper with those on the ground. When she was satisfied she had the map turned the right way, she said, "Maybe we shouldn't stay on the trail."

"What trail?" Mae asked.

She's right, Erin thought. It's rock on rock.

She checked the map again, her eyes moving over the slope. "We could zigzag through those boulders. It'd be faster too."

"A short cut?"

Erin tried to think clearly. "Looks like it."

"Okay. Boulders," Mae said, casting the deciding vote.

They choked down the last of the couscous.

Erin and Mae dipped their hands into a puddle of rainwater and washed their faces. Erin didn't bend over enough to see her reflection. She didn't need to know how bad she looked.

"Is it true some people get so hot they don't even sweat?" Mae said.

"Yep. It's called hyperthermia." Erin passed the bottle, wiping at the sweat tickling her neck. "And if your body temperature drops too low you won't even shiver. That's hypothermia."

"It's hotter than blazes during the day out here," Mae said. "Then we freeze to death at night."

"Think about John Muir. He didn't have all the high-tech clothes and gear."

Mae glanced down at her clothes, mud washed and sun dried. "Like tank tops?"

Erin tried a smile.

They'd only stopped for fifteen minutes, but it was too long. The sweat on Erin's body had cooled. She could barely drag herself to her feet. Her whole body was tight and stiff. Dirt clung to her like lichen on boulders.

They hiked on.

The only sound was the creaking of their packs and the crunch under their tattered sneakers as they scrambled over loose rock. Higher up, the ridge ran at tree line beyond barren peaks, vast spaces without a single stump.

"Muir knew everything about these mountains," Erin said, biting into a cracker. It tasted like splinters. "My grandma says he's the father of the national park system. If it weren't for him, all the trees around here would've been cut down and hauled away for lumber."

Mae took the lead through the maze of boulders, Sequoia at her side.

Erin took another drink and the cracker turned into a dough ball.

The slope rose gently, speckled with purple flowers. Larkspur. Poisonous to people and cattle.

Another hour fell behind them.

The air along the down-sweeping slopes was still. Too still, Erin thought.

She stopped where a fallen tree made a low stool. "What's wrong?" Mae asked.

"Blister." Erin sat down and took off her sneakers. The shoes looked like they were made out of mud. The big toe on her left foot poked through a hole in her sock. The skin had rubbed itself bloody. She thought about the lost first aid kit.

"What're you going to do?" Mae said.

"Chop it off," Erin answered.

It took Mae a second to realize Erin was joking. She laughed, then tore off a strip of material from one of the bandannas and wrapped Erin's toe.

"Thanks." Erin put her socks and sneakers back on and stood up, looking back down the mountain. The river twisted across the valley floor. Flowering plants with unfolding petals rooted in the fissures of rocks. Across and higher up the valley, belts of glacier-scored rock glistened in the setting sun.

Mae's chapped lips spread into a smile. "Awesome."

"Wish I had a camera," Erin said.

"It makes me feel so small, but not in a bad way," Mae said. "More like—I don't know—like there are bigger things than what's going on in my life to worry about."

Erin nodded. Even Lannie seemed farther away now.

"Wanna take a break?" Mae asked.

Erin shook her head. "Let's keep going."

She and Mae had been in the mountains for four days. That was more than enough time for a letter to travel from Camarillo to Lee Vining. This letter would be different from the first one. She imagined each word neatly written on lavender-scented stationery. Lavender, Lannie's favorite perfume.

Dear Erin,

I'm searching for how to say I'm sorry in a way that has more meaning than those two simple words. I know that words can never return all that I stole from you in terms of the worry and sadness I brought into your world. I don't know how to make it up to you. Please believe me when I say I love you very much. I always have. I know words can't make up for what's happened. But I promise I'll be here for you from now on.

Love, Mom

Erin slid on a layer of sharp-edged rocks. It was scary to be mad and hurt and worried all at the same time. She pushed the imaginary letter out of her mind. It would never happen anyway.

A gust of wind dropped on her like a hawk on a mouse. Dried leaves swirled into a dirt funnel. There was a temporary lull, then another steady blast cut through the girls like a razor.

Erin and Mae steadied themselves on a ledge not much wider than their packs and added another

layer over their shirts. Tying Sequoia's dirty bandannas over their noses and mouths bandit-style, they
squinted against swirls of wind-borne dirt. There
were wounded trees everywhere. Most had scorch
marks from lightning strikes.

Erin tugged on her straps, limping over the
uneven ground. She licked her lips, chalky with grit.
It felt like someone had shoved her face-first in the
sand. The blister shot fiery sparks up her leg.
Another gust pitched her forward and she had to jog
to catch up with herself.

"If there's such a thing as an encyclopedia of bad
weather, we've had it all," Erin said.

"We haven't had an earthquake," Mae added
helpfully. "Yet."

CHAPTER NINETEEN

Fears vanish as soon as one is fairly free
in the wilderness.

—JOHN MUIR

The sun throbbed like a fever before fading
behind a blanket of dust.

Another day had passed.

"We'd better look for a place to stop for the night,"
Erin said. "It'll get dark fast after the sun goes
down."

They found a sheltered spot between two big
rocks where the ground was almost level and grate-
fully shed their backpacks. Erin scuffed away the
gravel with her shoe and spread out the ranger's
sleeping bag.

"It'd better not rain tonight," said Mae. "If it
storms again, we'll probably drown."

Erin was so relieved to take off her sneakers and
rest her festering toe, she didn't care about rain or
thunder or lightning. All she could think about was
lying down.

* * *

The midday sun told Erin they had been on the trail five or six hours since breakfast: shriveled slices of dried apple. Not enough to keep a red wiggler alive. When she saw Sequoia eating grass, she felt bad for yelling at him about the fish yesterday.

Mae headed out in front. It was slow going. So slow, Erin felt like they'd shifted into reverse. Mae stepped sideways through a long, narrow chute, squeezing past slimy black rocks. Sequoia drank noisily at a shallow pool.

On the far side of the passage, the walls opened to a granite buttress. The trail gradually dropped, then regained lost elevation.

Erin stopped to pant. She could have sworn they'd passed the same igneous slab an hour ago, but she knew they hadn't. Her pack weighed too much. Sadly she realized she was carrying the lighter one.

I should've left some of the stuff in camp, she thought. But they weren't going back. They were hiking all the way to Horseshoe Meadows.

"The girls have peaked 10,000 feet for the second time today," Mae mimicked an announcer on a TV survival show. "Can they continue on rations of beetle juice and fly wings? Stayed tuned…"

Erin would have added a line of her own, but she didn't have the strength. Since their last stop, she'd developed a blinding headache. Tiny black pinpoints of light danced at the edges of her vision. The first stage of Altitude Mountain Sickness. At the severely ill end of the AMS scale the brain swelled and ceased to function properly.

"It's okay to get altitude sickness," Gram had said once. "But it isn't okay to die from it. If you ever feel sick like that, Erin, get to a lower elevation."

Mae glanced over her shoulder. "You okay?"

Erin added aspirin to her wish list. Probably in the first aid kit, she thought, rubbing her temples.

"Headache?" Mae asked.

Erin nodded and set off an avalanche in her skull.

"I have aspirin in my makeup bag," Mae said.

Erin felt like hugging her.

Sequoia sprawled between the girls while they rested on a granite ledge. Erin sipped from her water bottle, subconsciously rationing it, then passed it to Mae. Mae took a miserly swig and recapped the bottle. "How's your toe?"

Erin closed her eyes, letting the aspirin do its job. "What toe?"

Thirty minutes later they were zigzagging down a short pitch to a plateau at 9,500 feet. Erin thought the shrubs looked like ugly faces. She half expected them to talk. Her shirt caught on one of them. She yanked it free, hearing it rip. She touched her arm and felt a trickle of blood. Ignoring it, she continued to put one mud-caked sneaker in front of the other.

The trail just went on and on. No matter how much Erin felt like giving up, she forced herself to keep going, stumbling over the broken ground, climbing over jarring heaps of rock. When they descended another five hundred feet the black pinpoints of light disappeared. At 8,500 feet the jackhammer in her head lessened to a dull ache.

Erin knew a search-and-rescue team had to be looking for them. Where were they? She imagined a dispatcher speaking into a two-way radio. "Two girls...Lost near Cottonwood Pass...We'll reconnoiter at Horseshoe Meadows Campgrounds..."

In the dirt cloud hovering over the ground she imagined search-and-rescue members in their cabins wrestling to pull on jeans and T-shirts. Volunteers scattering across the backcountry, arriving by car and on foot, mapping strategies, talking fast in rescue lingo, grabbing headlamps, emergency kits. Team members ducking beneath the rotor blades of a fleet of helicopters, pushing into helmets and gloves. Erin could almost hear the *thwack-thwack-thwack* as the choppers lifted and twisted sideways above the four-hundred-mile-long spine of the Sierra Nevada.

Erin didn't know how long she'd been daydreaming, but seemingly without warning their route slammed into a dead-end. Without a word she and Mae turned back, climbed again, and moved between two shoulders of granite. Soon they found themselves in a narrow gorge. Erin waited for Mae to say something about being claustrophobic. But she didn't utter one grumbling word.

Mae's getting tougher, Erin thought, moving her hand over the rough rock. Stronger.

Erin hated thinking about Gram frantic with worry. Was Lannie worried too? Would that make her care the way she used to? Make her want to come home?

At a shallow pool Mae shrugged out of the heavier pack. "Any iodine left?"

Erin dropped to a boulder and took off her sneakers. "A few tablets."

Mae filled the water bottle, added iodine, then rinsed out the filthy bandannas. She used one to clean the scratch on Erin's arm, rinsed it again, and dabbed at her own knee wound, now mostly a scab.

Erin let her sore feet sink into the pool of water, stirring up a cloud of swimming bugs. The greenish bubbles made an oily film around her ankles. Her big toe felt numb. She propped her feet on a rock, letting them dry in the sun. The blister on her toe had broken miles back. Even with the makeshift bandage, her toenail was turning black.

"A week ago these were my favorite shoes," Erin said. She opened her knife and sliced a hole in her sneaker. She put it on and wiggled her sorry-looking toe. "That's better."

May counted out pine nuts and divided them in half. "We'll save the rest for dinner," she said, shoving what was left in her pocket.

Erin stood up and shouldered the heavier pack. "Tasty."

They hiked on, munching pine nuts and passing the water bottle back and forth. Small glacial lakes shimmered in a valley below, linked by a glittering stream. Further west, striking granite towers rose from a sloping mass of rock fragments broken off from the cliffs.

It's so desolate here, Erin thought as the wind roared down on them. No good place to camp. Not a single tree.

Step after step, Erin and Mae hunched against the wind, leaning forward, putting one shabby sneaker in front of the other. The wind was so strong it was impossible not to swallow dirt, even though they were both wearing bandannas. Violent gusts slapped them into rocks.

Erin counted her steps to lose track of time and distance. The amount of dirt-dust amazed her. The stuff drifted in and hung in the air, like a choking fog.

It took an hour to put the worst of the trail behind them. Eventually the walls flared to a steep saddle of broken shale. Now they could see trees: Pines on the opposite ridge packed together like arrows.

Mae pulled off her bandanna. "How long until we're out of here?" she asked, spitting grit.

Erin wasn't sure how many miles Horseshoe Meadows was from this ridge. She had originally thought they could hike out in one day. But that was two days ago. Distance kept tricking her.

"I'm not sure," she said as another blast threw her

sideways into the rock. The ranger's pack cushioned the blow, but threw her off balance. And I'm not sure how long we can last out here, she thought.

"Where's Sequoia?" Mae asked.

"I hope he's finding fresh water," Erin said unsteadily. "And a trail."

"Smart dog—" the rest of Mae's words were lost to the wind.

They plodded on, picking their way up a dozen narrow ledges. Erin noticed that Mae constantly tugged on the waist of her pants, trying to pull them up. Erin's cutoffs were floating on her too. She looked down and saw her hipbones jutting out above the waistband.

Somewhere above them came the sound of trickling water. The girls crept forward onto rocks black with seepage. Their shoes skated on the ooze-covered ledges, picking up a layer of slime.

Halfway up the wet rocks, they had to start climbing with their hands and feet. Soon they were using their knees and elbows too. A sharp rock found the hole in Erin's sneaker and a Roman candle went off in her foot.

It wasn't safe to stop now.

Erin thought about the ranger, wondering how he'd broken his ankle. What had finally killed him? Stop it, she told herself. Thinking about how someone died only makes things worse.

Mae called, "Can you write a song about slime?"

Erin laughed and slipped, nearly losing her footing. "Careful!" Mae shouted.

Another hundred yards further, they stopped on a narrow ledge for a much-needed rest. Erin forced herself to look at her sneaker. A pinkish-red stain spread out from the hole she'd cut. Mae's bandage had fallen off. Erin used her knife to cut a strip of material from her shirt. Then she stuffed it in the hole so she wouldn't have to look at the bloody mess.

Mae squatted on the ranger's pack. "How's your toe?"

"Better," Erin lied. She hoped the pain wouldn't slow them down.

"Hungry?" Mae asked.

"Old dried fruit sounds good."

Mae tossed her a shriveled apple slice. "Fresh from the tannery."

Mae scrubbed her slimy shoes with clumps of grass. Now she had a nasty cut on her elbow, as swollen and purple as yesterday's thunderheads.

Erin soaked a bandanna and washed Mae's wound. "Does it hurt?"

Mae shook her head. "Just a little."

They ate dried fruit and studied the map. "From where we are, here," Erin said, pointing, "it's only a couple of hours to the ridge."

Mae leaned in for a better look. "The Pacific Crest Trail?"

"Yeah."

Mae smiled. "It's about time."

Their eyes followed the lines on the map from the Pacific Crest Trail across the zigzag of ridge to Cottonwood Pass. Neither of them wanted to talk about the obvious. If they were where they thought they were, the trail would take them past the spot where the lightning had stuck. At least they'd be closer to Horseshoe Meadows Campgrounds and a pay phone.

Erin wondered if the dead horse and mule were still there. She hoped they'd both been buried. Then she thought about the poor ranger. Had someone found the pine cross at the cave?

After resting, Erin could barely stand up. Her whole body was stiff and sore. It felt like someone was holding a welding torch against her foot, constantly turning up the flame. She looked for a walking stick, but only scrawny trees grew in the thin soil. None were within reach.

Sequoia bounded onto the ledge looking like a drowned rat. He shook himself off, showering them with dirty water. He sniffed the slice of cheese Mae offered and turned it down. Mae shrugged and popped it into her mouth.

"He must've found something else to eat," Erin said. "Probably some poor squirrel."

Mae drew the dog into a wet hug. "Don't say that."

They headed out again, climbing up an abrupt ridge. Beyond it, the ground fell away in a gentle slope. Sequoia scampered ahead. Another fifty yards and the angle of rock tilted. Patches of dirt broke up the stony wall.

"It's too steep," Erin said. "Unless we can find cracks for our hands and feet."

Erin searched for signs of Sequoia's path.

Mae sighed. "I'd rather die than waste a day back-tracking."

Erin scanned the bleak rock face. It was nearly vertical in pitch. "If we had a rope one of us could climb to the top and hoist the packs up. But I don't think we can climb with the extra weight tugging on us."

Mae stared at the sheer rock. "We have to try."

CHAPTER TWENTY

When you get into a tight place and everything goes against you, till it seems as though you could not hang on a minute longer, never give up then, for that is just the place and time that the tide will turn.
—HARRIET BEECHER STOWE

The heat was intense under the glare reflecting off the granite. Erin figured that the wall was about as high as the gymnasium at her school. She mapped a route in her head while she and Mae ate pine nuts and sipped water. Both of their stomachs growled, but neither of them complained. Words couldn't make up for the lack of food.

Erin fixed a course firmly in her mind. "I'll go first."

"Why?" Mae demanded.

"It's safer that way."

"I'm in just as good shape as you are," Mae shot back. "Maybe better."

Erin had a tough time answering. She thrust her arms in the straps of the ranger's pack and hefted it. "The strongest person always brings up the rear," she mumbled. It hurt to admit Mae was the stronger one now.

"Are you making that up?"

Erin shook her head. "What if you were on top and I needed help? It'd be nearly impossible to climb down without a rope."

Mae thought about it. "Then I carry the ranger's pack."

Erin sucked up her pride. "Okay."

They quickly switched the knife and quick-release ring to the smaller pack.

Erin took her first steps on a series of rocky ledges. A few feet up she found a crack wide enough to support her sneakers. It took forever to go ten feet. She rested with one foot higher than the other and jammed in a cleft.

She struggled for balance, ignoring the pain stabbing her toe. She stretched her arms out against the granite wall.

"You look like a crossing guard," Mae called up.

That was exactly how Erin felt, like she was trying to stop traffic in every direction. The air closed in around her, as warm and clammy as dog breath. She followed the slanting crack, every slow step an agony. The fear of falling kept her hunched forward. She worked her way further along the ledge and glanced down—a sickening blur of twenty feet. She told herself not to look down again.

"Steady!" Mae called.

Erin tried to say something back—but her tongue lay like a slab in her mouth. Her dry lips stuck to her teeth. She pressed her cheek against cold rock, her spine taut as wire. If the angle got any steeper...she didn't want to think about turning back.

She set off again.

The heat from the sun scorched the top of her head. Her back dripped sweat. Her shirt hung on her like an old dishtowel.

She reached for a handhold, her fingers fat as boxing gloves. The scrapes on her knuckles throbbed and stung with sweat. She sucked her lips. Salt. In one push, she lifted herself to the left. Halfway into her next step something dark rushed down at her.

"Rocks!" Mae yelled up.

Erin froze, terrified. Heavy blows thudded against her shoulders, whacking her pack. Then it was past.

The rocks had missed her head.

"Are you okay?" Mae hollered.

Erin nodded. "The pack took most of it," she called back. Stay focused, she told herself. Or you're dead.

The angle of the crack opened to a foot-wide ledge. Erin pushed herself into it, panting. Her heart pounded so loud it hurt her ears. Her lungs felt like they were going to burst. But nothing was as bad as the pain in her toe.

"There's a knob above your right hand," Mae said. "You can reach it."

Erin leaned into the rock. Her fingers inched upward. She found the knob and another foothold and crept forward. Then she discovered several solid holds in a row.

"No free falls now!" Mae shouted.

Some joke, Erin thought. Was that supposed to make her feel better?

The wall was hot as an oven with the door left open. Sweat poured off her body. She pulled herself up and rested. Then boosted again. On a two-inch lip she hesitated, motionless. All she could think of was how good it would feel to stand on solid ground.

"Another ten feet!" Mae yelled.

Erin found a place for her left foot and pushed. Another hold for her right foot. Push. Pull. Push. That's it. She groped for another knob, feeling smooth stone. A short panting struggle and another step was behind her.

Erin realized she was thinking with her fingers more than her brain. The stink of her sweat steamed like a cloud. She just about choked on it. A fly zoomed in on her. There was no way to swat it. Even her hands sweated. She felt herself slipping and the chilling sound of fingernails scraping rock battered her ears.

Then there was no sound. Not even the wind. The dirty brown haze left the sky. The sun hung like a giant lantern.

"Erin!" Mae called.

Erin squeezed her eyes shut, hearing her name in the gray distance. One foot slipped. It pedaled air. She kicked out, opening her eyes.

"Erin!" Mae called again.

Suddenly the horizon tilted.

Erin shifted her weight.

"Are you okay?" Mae shouted.

Was she? Erin had no idea.

She dug into the rock with her knees. Her clothes had been loose all day, practically falling off. Now they fit tight and stiff, washed and ironed with mud. She noticed every fleck of quartz in the rock. Rose-pink, amber, slate gray. Shiny, like someone had polished them with an oiled sock. She saw herself in a square of silver. Then the colors blurred.

"You're almost there!" Mae hollered.

Erin pulled herself up. Her mind pushed her body aside and took over. Each hand searched blindly, edging its way into a crack deep enough for her fingers. She tried to take another step. Something pulled against her. She struggled, imagining herself dropping. Growing smaller and smaller. A speck of dust in the vast landscape.

If she fell she'd hit rock.

There wasn't anything else down there.

Stop it! Erin told herself.

She yanked again. With horror she realized her knife was jammed in a crack.

I should have put my knife inside the pack, she thought. She pulled on it, but the more she struggled the more tightly it became wedged.

"What's wrong?" Mae's voice had a panicky edge.

Erin couldn't answer. She wiggled again, twisting her body. She tried again. Failed. The struggle had worn her out physically, but the hardest part was coming to terms with her sagging spirit. She wanted to scream, to shock herself into action. Her throat wouldn't open.

Finally a raspy shriek burst out of her. "No!"

"What is it?" Mae yelled.

Erin stared at a fleck of quartz as if she might find something in the rock to contradict what she knew was true.

"I'm stuck." She said it without moving, almost without breathing. She gasped for what might be her last breath.

"What?" Mae sounded frantic now. "Erin, I can't hear you!"

Erin felt her pulse beating between her eyes. All of a sudden she didn't know the difference between up and down. *Vertigo.* That's what Gram said sometimes happened to people skiing in a whiteout blizzard—they lost all sense of direction.

Tears burned her eyes, clouding her vision.

She blinked.

Hard.

If she cried now, she'd die.

CHAPTER TWENTY-ONE

*I'm glad I did it, partly because it was well worth it,
but mostly because I shall never have to do it again.*
— MARK TWAIN

Erin didn't know how long she'd been clinging to
the rock—fifteen minutes, fifteen hours—but the
sweat on her body had dried. The air was so thick
you could shovel it. The fingers on her right hand felt
sticky. Blood. She shifted again, shivering. Her toe
had probably fallen off by now.

"Ditch the pack!" Mae called from below.

Erin squeezed her eyes shut. She was hanging
from a hairline crack.

"Take it slow."

Erin wiggled again.

She twisted sideways.

Failed.

"The knife's stuck!" Erin shouted.

"Try!"

Erin stared at the shadows on the ground and
struggled to clear her head. Gradually the pounding
in her heart quieted. So did the burning in her lungs.
She knew she couldn't hang on much longer. One

wrong move and she'd fall to earth. Lie there quietly. Sleep forever.

"Don't give up!" Mae yelled.

Erin fought back, hugging the rock. She tried to shrug off a strap. The pack refused to let go. She slipped, barely regaining her grip. Her stomach went into a free fall.

"Hang on!" Mae called. "I'm coming up!"

She wanted to shout, *No! It's too risky!* But Mae was her only chance.

Erin clung to her spot, her cheek pressed against the cold wall. Her breathing came faster, panic squeezing her chest.

Mae *is* a lot stronger now, she thought. Tougher.

Her mind suddenly became calm, as if part of her had lifted out of her body and she was watching herself from above. For a moment she forgot where she was. With her eyes closed, she slowly came back to reality. "Follow my route," she told Mae.

No answer.

"Mae?"

Still no answer.

Mae was either lost in concentration or consumed by panic.

Erin willed her on. *Come on, Mae. You can do it.*

From the corner of her eye, Erin saw her friend moving gracefully, like a great spider stretched across a web. Mae teetered on a fist-sized knob beside the lodged backpack, nail clippers in her mouth. Bracing herself, she reached out and wiggled the pack.

Erin slipped, barely holding on.

Fear came and went.

Mae worked the clippers. "I'm cutting the ring."

"Hurry," Erin whispered weakly.

Snap!

The quick-release ring holding the knife broke. Erin struggled to pull herself the rest of the way up the cliff face. First her head, then her shoulders. Her body moved like a rag doll over the last lip, her stomach scraping rock. She couldn't breathe. She stood up and immediately fell down. She lay on her pack, groping for breath.

Finally, she wiggled free of the pack. Every part of her body sank into the ground. She stared unblinking at the sky. Mae had been so wrong. Mother Nature really did care about them. "Thank you," she uttered.

Mae tossed the knife to Erin.

Then the two of them lost it: laughing and crying and hugging each other.

Sequoia licked their faces.

"He smells like rotten meat," Mae said.

"Must've found something dead to roll in."

Sequoia smiled his doggie smile.

Erin turned over and scooped water from a shallow pool, not caring about algae, giardia, or which animals might have used the pool for a bathroom. It tasted delicious, germs and all. She drank from her hands, taking in their surroundings. Beyond the granite crown a line of rugged pinnacles towered. Scores of peaks stood below them; others rose to their level.

A jagged skyline to the west marked ridges that seemed endless, especially in the thick, shadowy air. Yet they had somehow managed to scramble up one of the steeper slopes.

"It's a wasteland out here," Mae said. She dug the last pine nuts from her pocket and shared them with Erin. "Now I know where they got the names Forgotten Canyon and Siberian Outpost."

"And Bloody Gulch," Erin added.

"Let's call the rock we just climbed The Grateful Undead," Mae said. "How much time do you think we saved coming this way?"

Erin sighed. "We lost a couple of hours."

Mae grinned. "Is that all?"

Erin pulled out the piece of cloth she'd stuffed in the hole of her sneaker. Her toe looked like raw hamburger. She'd lost the nail.

Mae made a face. "Does it hurt?"

"The nail will grow back." Erin let her foot soak in the icy water until it grew numb. Then she soaked a bandanna strip and wrapped her toe.

Mae cut a bigger hole in the sneaker.

Biting her lip, Erin slipped her shoe on.

They walked side by side along a narrow ridge

that overlooked miles of gray desolation. Even the trees were knobby and bleached ashen. There wasn't any dirt up here. Just a rubble of stone on stone.

Erin pushed herself forward by counting the lichen splotches on the rock slabs. "Alice Algae and Freddy Fungi took a *lichen* to each other," she said, surprised she remembered the saying. "They've been on the rocks ever since."

Mae rolled her eyes. "That's the dumbest thing I've ever heard."

Erin realized the sky was much darker now, an iron gray between dusk and darkness. Soon shadows would squash them like cockroaches.

"No matter how hard we wish nighttime would stay away," she told Mae, "it keeps coming back."

CHAPTER TWENTY-TWO

...the sun is already in the west,
and soon our day will be done.
— JOHN MUIR

Erin and Mae hiked across loose shale for another hour, their long shadows trailing behind them. The sun touched the westerly rim of rock and exploded like a firecracker. Then the sparks faded.

Mae picked up the pace, as if speed could put off the end of the day. Sequoia scratched himself against a jagged rock, then trotted ahead. Erin limped behind them, trying to keep up. A scorpion in the trail shook its poisonous tail at her.

Mae stood still and waited. "How's your toe?"

Erin tried to shrug but the pack wouldn't let her. "It's still there."

She slumped on a boulder and shared the last bit of chocolate. She picked a dead ant off a melted glob, then realized she should have eaten it. *Protein.* Mae was licking her fingers like a toddler. Erin gazed at her hands. Even in the fading light she could see blood crusted around her nails, ragged from the rock climb.

Mae took the lead again.

Determined not to fall behind, Erin pushed on. Then the pounding in her head returned. Nausea churned her stomach. The bite of chocolate threatened to reappear. She should have adjusted to the altitude by now. After all, they were going *down*.

"We're traveling too fast," Erin said.

Mae swung around. "What's wrong?"

Erin choked on the bitter stuff in her throat. "Sick to my stomach."

Mae took it slower.

Erin staggered on, stopping every dozen steps, dropping her head between trembling knees. Her steps jerked over the irregular ground. She stopped, started, stopped. She wanted to die.

"Just throw up," Mae said finally. "You'll feel better."

Erin leaned over and let it go. Not much came up. Mae wet a bandanna and handed it to her. Erin wiped her mouth, feeling halfway human again. The pounding in her head quieted.

The night struck hard. No wind, no clouds, no movement of any kind. The trees far down the slope blended together into a dark mass.

"We can't camp here," Erin said. "There isn't any shelter."

Mae pulled out the ranger's map and flashlight, running a grubby finger over the twisting lines. "It looks like—" Mae glanced at Erin. "Do you think...?"

Erin nodded. "The Pacific Crest Trail."

"We're on it? You're sure?"

"As sure as I can be in the dark," Erin said.

"We have a flashlight."

Erin knew what Mae was thinking. "You don't want to stop?"

Mae returned her gaze. "I'm not tired."

"Are you sure?"

Mae nodded.

Erin thought they could make it. *Together* they could make it. "Let's go."

Mae swept the overgrown trail with the flashlight. They walked so close to each other Erin could hear Mae breathing. Sequoia stayed beside them for a change. They steadily picked up their pace, knowing Cottonwood Pass was within a few hours' hike.

"We're really bookin' it," Mae said.

Erin felt better since she'd thrown up. "Smokin'."

"What do you think happened to our search party?" Mae asked.

Erin didn't have a clue. "They must be out here somewhere."

They hiked on.

The beam of the flashlight cut through murky shadows. Hiking at night wasn't so bad, not after what they'd been through. A half hour sank behind them. Then an hour.

Mae pointed at a blurry shape on the trail ahead. "What's that?" she whispered.

Erin took a step, her eyes shifting. The dark shapes split in two and grew larger. She wondered if she was dreaming—the kind of dream you have when you're half asleep and half awake. She tugged on her straps to make sure she was standing up.

"I don't know what it is," Erin said.

Sequoia growled.

Mae grabbed his bandanna collar. "Shhh!" she told him.

Erin stopped walking to give her heart a chance to slow down. Two pinpoints of light were heading toward them.

CHAPTER TWENTY-THREE

Saying nothing...sometimes says the most.
— EMILY DICKINSON

Erin's gaze moved to a spot in the trail where granite closed in, creating a bottleneck. Two people stood in the narrow space. At least she thought they were people. She couldn't make out more than lumbering shadows beyond the glow of flashlights.

Even though she couldn't see them, it felt like they were staring at her. The hikers walked closer.

Erin swallowed hard.

She wasn't afraid. Just startled. After all these days, all these miles, it was such a shock to see people. They were about thirty feet away now. Huge packs towered a foot above their heads, casting shadows across their faces. One hiker, a lot taller than the other, stabbed at the ground with a walking stick. Both wore shorts, heavy fleece pullovers, sturdy boots.

After all this time wondering why they hadn't seen a rescue team—or anyone with food and supplies—now Erin didn't know if she wanted help.

Cottonwood Pass was less than an hour away and on a straightforward trail. Horseshoe Meadows stood a few miles down the switchback from there.

"Bet they have a tent," Mae whispered.

"Food," Erin whispered back.

"Sleeping bags."

"Toothpaste."

"Do you think they know who we are?" Mae said in a hushed voice. "That we've been lost?"

"I don't know," Erin answered.

The hikers moved closer. The person on the left stepped forward and lowered his flashlight. A tall man, well muscled. About her dad's age. A pair of sunglasses hung on a cord around his neck.

Erin wanted to blurt out, "Do you have any extra food? We haven't had anything to eat in—" She couldn't remember if it had been five days or five weeks. Her stomach pinched her. Not a dream. She had a strange impulse to ask them if they had any cookies.

Instead, she took a step back. She wasn't sure she wanted to get into a conversation with these guys.

The shorter man spoke first. "You two girls out here alone?"

Erin didn't answer. But she didn't look away either. She shifted her pack, trying to stand taller. She wanted to look older. "Our parents are behind us," she said at last.

Mae shot her a shocked look.

The first man stared at them, eyebrows raised. "How far back?"

"Not far," Mae added quickly.

"You should've stayed together," he said. "Anything can happen in the dark."

Mae pretended to think about it. "You're right. We're—"

"We were going to wait for them up ahead," Erin put in. She felt strange telling lies like this, one after another, as if she'd been doing it her whole life.

"We camped at Chicken Springs Lake last night," the short guy said, sounding friendly enough. "Got a late start this afternoon. Any good places to pitch a tent close by?"

Erin wasn't about to tell them she and Mae had just scaled a granite wall without a rope, harness, or helmets. They probably wouldn't believe her anyway. "The ridge is rocky," she said. "No place to set a stake."

The tall guy stepped closer. "Did you and your family hike in from Sequoia?" he asked.

Sequoia barked at his name. Mae held him tighter.

Erin knew he meant Sequoia National Park, more than 400,000 acres of mountain wilderness. That was the direction she and Mae should have been coming from—the western slope of the Sierra Nevada.

"Part way," Erin said.

The guy with the sunglasses chewed on Erin's answer. She noticed his eyes were deep set, unwavering. She figured he was wondering about their tattered clothes and beat-up appearance.

"Maybe we'd better hang out with you for a while," he said.

The shorter man frowned, little worried creases around his eyes. "Until your parents get here."

Sequoia barked again, pulling against Mae's hold.

Erin stood still, silence spinning around her.

Lannie used to use that worried tone.

How long ago?

Years.

Tucked in the back of Erin's mind were memories of Lannie: Sewing costumes for school plays. Singing too loud in church. Reading *Where The Wild Things Are* until they both fell asleep.

That was before she went crazy.

Crazy?

The idea threw Erin off balance.

The beam from the guy's flashlight jiggled and jerked, nearly blinding Erin when it swung across her face. "You sure you two aren't out here by your-selves?" the man asked again.

"No," Mae said firmly. "We aren't alone."

CHAPTER TWENTY-FOUR

*It takes a lot of courage to show
your dreams to someone else.*
—ERMA BOMBECK

The man asked a few more questions. Erin and Mae must have given him the right answers, because he and his companion eventually decided to keep going.

The girls watched the two men pick their way down the trail by the light of their flashlights. The figures became a dim fog before their edges completely disappeared in a gray mist.

"I wasn't lying when I said we weren't alone," Mae said.

Erin smiled. "We're together."

The mist turned to rain and the girls hurried to put on long pants and sweatshirts. They tied the shredded garbage bags over their heads and hiked down a series of zigzags that turned back on themselves, passing widely spaced pines. At the bottom the trail was nearly flat, only a few ups and downs. Knowing they were so close to Cottonwood Pass eased the hollow pain in their stomachs. Erin wasn't even limping much.

"I wonder if it would've been different if we'd been camping," Mae said.

Erin had thought about that too. "You mean if we'd planned it?"

"Yeah."

"Gram says the definition of an adventure is an experience outside your comfort zone."

"Guess we had an adventure then," Mae said.

They didn't slow down until they reached the section of the trail where the horse and mule had been killed. Erin fanned the flashlight over the water-logged ground. All evidence of the disaster had been lost to rain and mud.

Down the canyon a coyote yipped a secret code.

Sequoia howled back.

"What did they do with…" Mae began.

"Buried them, probably."

"Who did?" Mae's voice trembled.

"The rangers couldn't leave dead animals here." Erin shrugged. "Not on such a well-traveled trail."

The drizzle let up and a sliver of moonlight spread shadows on the trail. Erin loved this kind of moon—a quarter on its way to being full. The moon is something you can always count on, she thought. Strong enough to rule oceans. Just when you think it's gone it comes back stronger than ever.

The girls stuffed the garbage bags in their packs and hiked on. They picked up speed at the bottom of the switchback where the trail fanned into a sweeping meadow.

"Can I ask you something?" Mae said.

"No."

Mae ignored her. "What scares you most? Not counting being lost in the mountains."

Erin let the question wrap itself around her. She remembered the terrible stink of burning hair and almost said, Being hit by lightning. Then she thought of something worse.

"Okay...what if I visit Lannie? And she acts like everything is okay?" Erin said. "Like the last year never happened."

"Would she do that?" Mae asked.

"I can't pretend that everything is all right." Erin stared into the darkness, clutching the flashlight. "That's what we did before, even when Lannie acted so crazy."

She stopped and took a breath. *Crazy.* She'd finally said it aloud. She couldn't call it back. Her mother was crazy.

"It's okay," Mae murmured.

Erin nodded, biting her lip.

They continued to plod along, almost as silent as the old trees they passed. Erin let the beam of the flashlight brush the ground, making weird splotches in the dirt. Time didn't seem so important now. She supposed it was sort of like the river. One thing happened, then disappeared on the current. Something else took its place, only to be swept away too.

"What about you?" Erin said. "What are you most afraid of?"

Mae must have been thinking about that question because she answered quickly. "That I'll go back to being the way I was before—I'd hate that."

"Don't worry." Erin let herself smile. "I won't let you."

They made a pact to go camping together sometime with Gram.

"I can't wait to meet her," Mae said.

The girls wound their way through the dark woods, where the trees wavered in stark shadows just beyond the reach of the flashlight. Suddenly the glow of campfires fluttered in the distance like a bowl of goldfish: Horseshoe Meadows.

"I feel like I can handle anything now," Mae said.

Erin felt the same way. "We already have."

They definitely weren't the same as when they'd started five days ago.

Music filtered through the night air. "So much for pretending…" It was one of Erin's favorite songs. She softly sang the chorus, "Can't cry anymore…"

At the bottom of the switchback, the girls crossed the field by the parking lot. There was no Volkswagen. No U.S. Forestry van. Just a scattering of SUVs and trucks. They didn't stop until they reached the camp restrooms. A pay phone hung on the outside wall, lit by a gas lamp.

Erin dropped the ranger's pack near the bulletin board posted with bear warnings and campground rules. She spotted the TWO MISSING GIRLS flier right away. She scarcely recognized the girls in the pictures. They looked so...*clean*. "Mae," she said, stepping closer. Their names and birth dates were printed beneath each photograph, along with a line telling where the girls had last been seen. "Look, it's us."

Mae sighed. "Guess we're more important than a fleabite after all."

"Yeah," Erin said.

"We'd better call home," Mae said, then dug some change from her knapsack. "Call your grandmother first."

"What about your parents?" Erin asked.

Mae gave Erin the money. "First I'm going find some scraps for Sequoia."

Erin stood in the half-shadows watching Mae walk toward the campfires. Sequoia followed, wagging his scruffy tail. Mae barely resembled the girl who'd started out on a hike nearly a week ago, she thought. Her face was sunburned and scratched and her clothes were little more than rags. Erin doubted anyone would recognize her.

Erin rolled dimes and quarters in her hand, thinking about the mountains, everything she and Mae had gone through. It felt like she was reliving years, not days.

She pushed the coins into the phone and dialed.

The phone rang.

She imagined Gram rushing barefoot through the kitchen. The phone kept ringing.

Pick it up, Gram, she willed.

"Hello?" Gram sounded far away, like a bee in a knothole.

"Gram!"

"Erin?" Her voice was anxious. "Is that you?"

"Gram!" Erin repeated.

Her mind was a swollen river, raging downhill over rocks, bouncing around bends, shifting direction. "I...we..." She wanted to tell Gram everything all at once.

Gram hushed her. "There's time for that later," she said. "Where are you?"

"Horseshoe Meadows."

"I'll call the sher—"

Erin interrupted, "Oh, no, Gram." She didn't want to be picked up by a stranger in a uniform. *"Please..."*

"I have to call and let them know you're safe." Erin pictured Gram's eyes, rock-steady. "But I'll pick you up myself, little bird."

* * *

Erin clung to the receiver, wondering if she had said good-bye. She pictured Gram slipping on her sheepskin boots, pushing through the rusty screen door. The pickup was always parked in a clump of weeds by the porch. The keys were kept in the ashtray.

She hung up the phone, then went inside the bathroom, surprised at how strange the concrete felt under her feet. Solid and flat. A dust-coated bulb was screwed into the ceiling. The stink was overwhelming. Then she realized she was smelling herself.

Erin saw a painting over the sink. *Why would someone hang a picture in here?*

The portrait showed a girl with hollow cheeks. Her eyes were much too big for her face, rimmed with gray circles. Her face was held together with crusty scratches. Her hair tumbled around her shoulders like a dirty mop.

Erin thought the girl had a faraway look: sad, lost, scared. She noticed something else about the eyes. They were empty, like the girl had forgotten how to use them. They were like Lannie's eyes. But rounder, darker. She traced the face with her finger.

For a moment Erin lost her boundaries. The cold slab walls were her arms and legs. The flickering bulb became a beating heart. Then she recognized the filthy sweatshirt.

She was looking in a mirror.

Erin stared at the image and wondered what it would be like to be inside Lannie looking out, instead of the other way around. What would it be like to go days without sleeping? Can that make someone crazy?

Then she wondered how long Lannie had thought about leaving. She had to have planned it. Packed. Hired a van. All in secret.

"Why couldn't you tell us what was wrong?" Erin

asked Lannie in the mirror. Her breath made a circle of steam on the glass that dissolved the image.

On Erin's thirteenth birthday, Gram had taken her to buy a real bra. That night Erin found a large envelope under her pillow. Inside was an arty photo her dad had shot of a woman in a hospital bed cradling a baby. Even though Lannie wore a bathrobe and her hair was a mess, her smile said, *Hey, take our picture!*

Erin had slipped the photo under her mattress, wondering if Lannie would ever hold her again.

Still staring at herself in the mirror, Erin felt in her pocket for the angel earrings. Miraculously, they were still there.

CHAPTER TWENTY-FIVE

Music was my refuge. I could crawl into the space
between my notes and curl my back to loneliness.
— MAYA ANGELOU

Mae stepped from the flickering shadows, trailed by Sequoia. The dog was gnawing on a meaty bone. "I got brownies too, Erin," she said, holding up a bag.

Erin ate her share so fast she nearly choked.

"You wouldn't believe these campsites," Mae said, licking chocolate off her fingers. "Get this. The people who gave me the brownies had a tablecloth and flowers. Bet they couldn't have survived without a tent."

Erin stared into the parking lot. "Let's hope they never have to find out."

"How did we ever make it?" Mae shook her head.

"Fear," Erin said. "The mother of invention."

"Well, none of it was easy."

Erin shrugged. "What is?"

"Did you call home?" Mae asked.

"Gram's on her way." Erin smiled. "Your turn."

Mae knelt by Sequoia, whispering to him as if

sharing some great secret. She seemed to be studying something in the distance where light from the camper's lanterns attracted bugs. She drew him into a hug and buried her face in his smelly coat.

Erin knew how hard it was going to be for Mae to give him up. She touched Mae's shoulder. "My parents are going to kill me," Mae said. "But I guess I can't put off talking to them."

"We're safe. They won't care about anything else."

"Think so?"

Erin gave her a reassuring squeeze. "Know so."

Mae looked doubtful.

Erin handed Mae the rest of the change.

Mae went to the phone and dropped in the quarters. She dialed, listened for several seconds, and hung up.

"No answer?" Erin asked.

Mae jammed her hands in her pockets. "It's busy."

"Call again in a few minutes."

"What if I can't get through?" Mae asked.

"You can go home with me," Erin said. "Call from there."

"Okay. Thanks." Mae pulled a burr from Sequoia's fur. He stayed close to her even when she wasn't feeding him.

Erin shined the flashlight on the ranger's torn map, piecing it together. Using the pencil, she marked the route to the cave where they had found him. "The poor ranger," Erin said sadly.

"What should we do with his stuff?" Mae asked.

"Take it to the ranger's station."

"What about Sequoia?" she asked, her voice unsteady.

Erin felt bad for her. Really bad. "Jake's lucky to get his dog back—he'll be grateful you took such good care of him."

Mae looked as miserable as Erin felt.

Erin scratched the dog's scruffy head. "I'm gonna miss him too."

Mae nodded, biting her lip. She wadded up the bag that had held the brownies and put it in the trashcan. "Pack it in, pack it out," she said. "I told you I knew what it meant."

A cold wind blew at them from the west. It whistled through the pines scattered around the edge of the parking lot. Judging by the number of tents, there were only a dozen or so people in the campgrounds. The night air magnified their voices, making it sound like a big crowd. Music blared from a car in the parking lot. Even the light outside the bathroom was too intense.

Mae called home again. "Still busy. And I didn't get my quarters back this time. How long will it take your grandmother to get here?"

Erin calculated the distance from Lee Vining to the turnoff in Lone Pine. One hundred and fifty miles. Driving in the dark in the old pickup would take Gram about three hours. Then another twenty miles from Lone Pine, climbing up the narrow mountain road, the only road to Horseshoe Meadows. "Four hours," Erin said. "Maybe longer."

"Might as well try to get some rest, then," said Mae. The girls spread out the sleeping bag in a sheltered spot near the parking lot and settled in to wait. Sequoia curled up at their feet and immediately began to snore. One by one the campfires went out and the noise died down.

"Are you asleep?" asked Mae after a while.

"I'm too wired to sleep."

"How much longer do you think it'll take your grandmother to get here?"

"I don't know. Maybe another couple of hours?"

"I'm not going to sit here all that time." Mae got up. "Just waiting."

Erin stared at her.

"You have something against walking all of a sudden?" Mae asked.

"Heck no."

They rolled up the sleeping bag and stuffed it into the ranger's backpack. Mae shouldered the heavier pack, and the two girls headed down the only road leading out of the campground.

Away from the light of the campgrounds the moon was brighter. Stars swam in the sky. Erin switched off the flashlight. No cars passed, coming or going.

Erin and Mae walked close together. Maybe we

really can hike forever, Erin thought. She and Mae
had long since passed the point of exhaustion.

Their sneakers barely made a noise on the asphalt
road. There wasn't much sound at all, except the
squeak of their packs and the wind whispering
through the trees.

Sequoia stayed by Mae.

Erin limped, her toe throbbing.

"How far can we walk in an hour?" Mae's voice
cut through the dark. "On a road like this?"

Erin answered without turning her head. "Guess
we'll find out."

Gauzy clouds drifted in from the northwest,
swirling in front of the moon. Wind would follow.
Maybe even rain. That would be okay. The asphalt
road was too straight, too smooth. Rain would keep
them alert.

They trudged ahead through a drifting mist. Erin
watched the clouds change form. Suddenly she
stopped in the middle of the road and picked up a
rock. She closed her eyes feeling the surface. Cold
and hard. All the worrying, all the hunger.
Everything seemed to hit her at once. She opened her
eyes. The rock was still there.

The chilly night air seeped into her clothes.

That was real, too.

Erin threw the rock into the darkness, hearing the
dull thud when it hit the ground. "What if she wants
me to stay in Camarillo?"

"You mean live with Lannie?"

Erin stumbled over her own feet. She would have fallen if Mae hadn't caught her. "I never got to say good-bye. She was just gone. It's so unfair. Didn't she think about that? Didn't she think about me and Dad at all?"

Mae seemed to be absorbing Erin's words trying to figure out something comforting to say. "Maybe your mom was lost for awhile. You know, like us."

Erin stared at the dark road, trying to fit together pieces of her memories. Lannie shopping till the stores closed. Bursting into Erin's room loaded down with bags. Unloading stuff on Erin's bed: Thirty tubes of lipstick. Prenatal vitamins. Lotto tickets. Bowling shoes. Mouse traps. Lace bras in odd sizes.

Erin had hugged her pillow, wondering if Lannie would ever stop talking.

"You know," she said to Mae, "when Lannie first called about me coming to visit her in Camarillo, Gram said, *You have to go so you'll know.* Maybe she meant that I had to talk to Lannie myself. So I'd understand what happened—why she left."

Mae's eyes turned to her. "Maybe Lannie's okay now."

Erin looked past the painted lines down the road. The lines looked tired, faded, worn out. She felt tired too. Tired of worrying. Tired of crying in her sleep. Tired of blaming herself.

She thought about how scared she'd been eleven

months ago. Hiding up in the tree. Carving her initials in the bark. Now she felt the same burning knot in her stomach. "I never want to be that afraid again," she said.

"It isn't your fault that your mom left," Mae said softly.

"I know." Erin swallowed the lump in her throat, the ache settling in her chest. "But maybe I could have done something to make her stay."

"Like what?" Mae said.

"I don't know. I just want things to be the way they were before, when I was little." Erin kept walking. Quietly like she had in the mountains, deep in her own thoughts. Another half mile down the road, she started humming. Gradually she began to sing.

Walk with me.
Feel the sun on your back.
The rain on your face...

"That's cool," Mae said. "Is that a song you're working on?"

Erin shrugged. "Yeah. It'd sound better with a guitar."

"Teach it to me?" Mae asked.

Erin sang each word plainly, the notes full and bold:

It doesn't matter who you are,
mountains will bring you together.

Her voice softened on the last line. *Show me the footsteps of a friend.*

Mae sang too. *Show me the footsteps of a friend.*

It felt different singing her song with someone else.

"...*footsteps of a friend,*" Erin repeated the chorus. She felt calm now.

Together Erin and Mae limped along and sang and watched for the crooked headlights of the pickup truck.

CHAPTER TWENTY-SIX

To have courage for whatever comes in life—
everything lies in that.
—St. Teresa of Avila

The sound of the old pickup brought tears to Erin's eyes. She heard its loose muffler long before it rattled around the bend, casting its uneven headlights. The brakes squeaked and the truck stopped in the middle of the road.

For a few moments Erin and Gram stared at each other through the windshield. Then Gram climbed down from the cab, her silver hair a wild mass of waves from last night's braids. A loose cotton skirt danced around her sheepskin boots.

Erin collapsed into her sturdy arms. Gram hugged her back, full and strong. Her soft skin felt warm against Erin's cheek.

Erin smiled through every aching muscle.

* * *

Gram drove slowly down the steep grade, her chunky silver rings clanking against the steering wheel. Erin let herself sink into the worn seat and into her grandma, their legs pressing together, as if touching proved they were both real. Erin loved the closeness.

Gram pointed to a sack on the floorboard. "Wish I could say it was homemade."

Erin and Mae tore hungrily into barbecued chicken, ribs, coleslaw, rolls. They ate like wild animals, sucking sauce from their fingers, gulping noisily from milk cartons. They ate like they were afraid the food would disappear if they didn't swallow it fast enough.

Sequoia was sitting on a wooden crate in the space behind the seat. He kept whining for a bite. Mae fed him chicken she picked off bones. He gobbled it down, resting his head on her shoulder between bites.

"The more I eat the hungrier I get," Erin said.

"Slow down." Gram's eyes smiled in the rearview mirror. "Before you make yourself sick."

Erin only half-chewed the stringy meat, reaching for another rib before she finished the one in her hand. She stuffed a roll with globs of coleslaw and shoved the whole thing in her mouth at once. Mae couldn't slow down either. Their stomachs had minds of their own.

Gram turned on the wipers when rain slapped at the truck. Erin glanced at the speedometer. Twenty-five miles an hour? *Unbelievable.* It would've taken them days to go that far in the mountains. How far had they gone? she wondered. With all the zigzagging and backtracking it was impossible to figure out.

Gram stared straight ahead, taking the curves in low gear. The truck's headlights batted at trees along the road. "The sheriff turned over every tumbleweed on the highway," she said. "At first we thought you were hog-tied and snatched from the bus station."

Erin was shocked. She hadn't really thought about anything like that. She felt terrible about giving her grandmother such a scare.

"After they found the Discovery Bound group, though, the rangers and the sheriff put two and two together." Gram shook her head, her body sagging. "Levi told them he and his sister had picked up a girl named Erin about Mae's age."

Mae looked up. "Levi?"

"I've just about worn my ear out talking with your parents," Gram said. "We've all been worried to pieces."

"Really?" Mae asked.

Gram nodded. "Your pictures have been in all the papers—on TV too, the neighbors tell me. I hear crusty old Edgar Harold headed up a search party of his own—a dozen or so volunteers from around the county."

Erin warmed to the idea that people cared so much. "Are they still out there?" she said.

"I'm sure the sheriff has gotten word to everyone letting them know you're both safe," Gram answered.

They sat quietly for a while, listening to rain hit the roof of the truck. Below, scattered lights twinkled in Lone Pine. Some of them moved. Cars on the highway. The lights were beautiful, like candles on a cake.

Erin stared down at her shredded sneakers. Her big toe stuck out the hole. She hoped her toenail would grow back before school started in September.

These feet have gone a long way, she thought. I bet they still have a little struggle left in them. "Gram?" Erin murmured. "Did Lannie call?"

Gram nodded. "Of course. She's been as worried as the rest of us. Glued to the phone waiting for word you'd been found unharmed."

Erin sunk lower in the seat, realizing that's what she'd been waiting to hear.

"Lannie even got through to your father in Guatemala...finally," Gram said, letting the old truck speed up on the straightaways. "She said he got on the first plane back to the States."

Erin needed to talk to her dad so much her throat ached.

"*Lost,*" Mae muttered.

"We were definitely lost," Erin said.

Then she told her grandma about finding the ranger's body in the cave.

"What a shame," Gram said, shaking her head. "A crying shame."

* * *

The truck bounced through a pothole in the driveway beside the weathered farmhouse. The first thing Erin smelled trudging up the steps was the rust on the front porch swing. Then the spicy scent of rosemary and basil from the terra-cotta pots beside the door.

She dropped the ranger's pack on the top step. Gram gathered what was left of their clothes and headed to the washroom at the back of the house.

"Bet they could walk there on their own," Gram said.

Mae laughed. "What do you think was holding us up?"

Garbage bags and four ragged sneakers lay heaped in a pile. Erin knew the shoes were worthless, but she didn't want to throw them away. "Think I'll have them bronzed," she told Mae.

"Bookends." Mae petted Sequoia. "Could I use the phone? I have to call home."

Erin led the way to the kitchen.

Seeing Gram at the stove heating soup seemed so—Erin tried to think of the right word. *Normal* didn't fit. *Comforting*, maybe. Yeah, that was it. Gram had already given Sequoia a bowl of water.

"Mom!" Mae said into the phone, stretching the

cord to its limit. She kept repeating, "Calm down, Mom. We're okay…Really."

Erin busied herself helping Gram get the food to the table. Only two hours had passed since she'd eaten, but she was hungry all over again. She poured herself a bowl of homemade turkey soup and tore off a hunk of freshly baked bread, raking it through a tub of butter. Gram filled jelly jar glasses with milk. Under the table, Sequoia let out a low grumble as he wolfed down chunks of tuna.

Mae hung up and sat by Erin at the table. "I could hardly understand my mom," she said. "She was crying so hard. Dad got on the phone too. They're gonna drive down first thing in the morning. They want us to get some sleep."

"What about Levi?" Erin asked.

"He's still out there—part of a search party looking for us. They'll pack up and hike in as soon as the sun's up," Mae said. "Guess everyone was on the wrong wide of the mountain. "

"*We* were on the wrong side," Erin said.

Gram set out a plate of iced oatmeal cookies, big as hubcaps. "You know, they airlifted that cowboy off the mountain by helicopter."

"How?" Erin asked, surprised.

"During a break in the storm, I guess. They flew the Discovery Bound leader to the hospital in Lone Pine," Mae went on. "He's going to be okay. The kid who broke his arm too."

Gram took over the story. "The leader had X rays to make sure his organs weren't fried. They say being hit by lightning is like being zapped in one of those microwave ovens. Cooks you from the inside out. The sheriff told me they released him the next day. The boy too, after they set his arm."

"What about Jake?" Erin asked.

Mae looked scared all over again. "Mom said he's still in the hospital—he has to have surgery. The horse crushed his leg."

Erin cringed. "Geez."

Mae reached under the table and scratched the collie. He let out a low, happy whine. "Think he'll let me take care of Sequoia till he gets better?" she asked.

"I bet he'd be grateful," Gram said. "We'll get in touch with him tomorrow."

CHAPTER TWENTY-SEVEN

If you don't like something, change it;
if you can't change it, change your attitude.
—MAYA ANGELOU

M ae took her shower first and borrowed a flannel nightgown from Gram. Erin soaked in the hot tub, rubbing her tight, tired muscles. Then she put on baggy sweats and an extra large T-shirt of her dad's with a logo of a blues festival on the front. Her toe looked like a prune, brown and shriveled. She found antibacterial cream, adhesive tape, and gauze pads in the medicine chest.

Sequoia squirmed through his own bubble bath, then sat quietly on the porch while Mae brushed him dry.

It was nearly 3:00 A.M. when Erin and Mae crawled into bed.

Erin knew she should have been dead asleep as soon as she hit the cool sheets. But she thrashed around, unable to get comfortable. The bed was too soft. The sheets were too clean. She finally dropped to the floor with her pillow, covering herself with a blanket.

But she couldn't get comfortable on the floor, either. "Mae?" she whispered. "You asleep?"

Mae was breathing heavily, sprawled diagonally across the bed. Her arms were draped over Sequoia.

Erin ran her hand under the mattress until she found the envelope with Lannie's letter. Maybe I missed something, she thought. She read it once quickly, then again slowly, paying attention to the scribbles in the margins. Squares and triangles. Some were shaded in with colored pencil. Others sprouted scraggly-stemmed flowers.

She wondered what would happen if she planted the letter—stuck it in the dirt. Would it grow answers to all her questions about Lannie?

She felt for the angel earrings on her nightstand and put them on. She slipped from the blanket and headed toward the porch. The screened room was large and airy. No curtains. It smelled like potting soil and herbs. A good smell, moist and rich.

Outside, wind blew hard enough to make the leaves on the oaks whistle. The moonlight pushed its way through the screen. A cobweb glistened in a high corner. Erin curled up on the porch swing and listened to small animals skitter in the weeds.

Gram came through the door and moved across the floor, the hem of her plaid robe brushing the rough planks. "Erin," she began gently. "You spend too much time thinking."

Erin realized she was still clutching Lannie's letter.

Gram sat beside her on the swing and looked over at her cautiously. Her hair hung in thick night braids. "We thought your mother had some kind of nervous breakdown," she said. "We didn't know what else to call it. And we didn't know why it happened."

Erin felt herself shaking down deep where Gram couldn't see. "Why didn't anyone tell me?"

"How could we explain what we didn't know? Your dad made appointments with doctors, honey, but Lannie refused to keep them."

Erin focused on a hole in the porch screen and listened to the oak leaves rustling. The moon died behind clouds. Neither of them said anything for a long time.

Gram swallowed and tried again. "Sometimes it's hard to know the right thing to do."

Erin met Gram's eyes in the dim light. "I bet some people know the right thing and still don't do it," Erin said.

"Maybe, but they aren't part of this family." Gram covered Erin's hand with her own. "People do strange things when they're sick."

"You mean *crazy*."

"That's a harsh word, Erin. It shows no effort to understand." Gram's tone said she meant it.

Erin nodded, but she didn't apologize. She felt mad. Hurt. She felt like someone had pulled the plug on every memory of happiness she'd ever had and they all drained out.

"Your mother was in a hospital for awhile. Then a special home," Gram said. "She has a job now. Her own apartment. She's seems so much better."

"You didn't know where she was?"

"Not until she called," Gram answered. "And that's the truth."

Erin hesitated, trying to decide whether or not she should say what she was thinking. "Hospitals have phones."

"I'm not denying that."

Gram squeezed her hand, mashing the letter into a tight ball.

Erin looked down. One hand over the other. Two were so much stronger than one. Gram pulled her into a hug. The swing's hinges squeaked.

All at once Erin felt exhausted. She stared at her and Gram's hands. Her gaze wandered to her own tanned and battered arms.

She had lots of things to pick at—dead skin, scabs, bug bites. She had just as many questions to pick. Eleven months worth. Did Lannie know she was sick? Is that why she left? Was she confused? Ashamed?

The letter said, *I need to find myself.*

Could Mae have been right?

Had Lannie felt lost in her own home?

Erin bit a sliver of dry skin on her lip. "Why didn't you tell me, Gram? When she called last week? Before I got on the bus?"

"She wanted to tell you herself," Gram replied. Sitting side by side, Erin was as tall as her grandma. Their dark eyes met. "I thought Lannie was right about that. Maybe I was wrong. If so I'll be the first to admit it."

Erin felt her body let go.

Her mind suddenly quieted.

"So is she okay?" she asked.

"There isn't any cure for what Lannie has, if that's what you're asking." Gram said it straight out.

"No. I mean, is she calmer?" Erin asked. "You know, like before?"

"As long as she takes her medication she's stable," Gram said. "That's what Lannie intends to keep doing and I believe her."

Erin swallowed a yawn and stared out the screened windows. She didn't know what to think.

"Some things you have to try. Some things you have to do," Gram said. "And no one can tell you when it's time for one or the other."

It's so much harder to *do* than to *think*, Erin thought. "What should I do?" she asked aloud.

"No *shoulds* about it." Gram waved absently at a cobweb. "You take your time to figure things out."

Erin must have been shivering, because Gram got up and brought over another quilt. She tucked the thick folds around Erin's shoulders. "Better, little bird?"

Erin looked up.

Her grandma's face was thoughtful and soothing, but her body was sturdy as the wool robe. "Thanks, Gram," she said softly.

Gram kissed Erin on the cheek. "Sleep tight," she said and went inside.

"Don't let the bedbugs bite," Erin whispered after her.

CHAPTER TWENTY-EIGHT

Life is what we make it, always has been, always will be.
—GRANDMA MOSES

Morning.

For a second Erin didn't know where she was. She tried to focus on the pine branch ceiling in the shelter, listening for sounds of the river. Then she saw Mae curled up in a blanket on the porch floor and realized she was home in Lee Vining. Sequoia slept beside Mae.

They must not have able to sleep inside last night, either.

Erin scooted off the swing, careful not to make it squeak.

She didn't feel hungry, but she wandered into the kitchen anyway. It felt weird to walk without anything on her back or anything to carry. No flashlight, no water bottle. Just walking, she thought. Such a simple thing. So light. She'd never take it for granted again.

The clock on the stove blinked 5:22 A.M. It would start getting light soon. Erin bet Mae's family was already on the road.

She glanced around the kitchen. There were so many drawers. Cupboards. The refrigerator in the corner, a metal giant.

Erin set Lannie's letter on the counter and opened the pantry, grabbing food and stacking it on the table. All kinds of food. Boxes of cereal, crackers, jars of preserved fruit.

Hunger. Until those days in the mountains, she hadn't known what it meant to be really hungry.

From the refrigerator she snatched mayonnaise, oranges, relish, cheese, almonds, squash. Food that would ordinarily taste terrible together. Erin just wanted to look at it. She let her eyes feast on the variety. She pulled out a cold Mexican casserole and stabbed the rubbery cheese with a spoon.

Mae came in, wrapped in the blanket. "Save some of that for me."

Erin grinned and handed her a fork.

They sat at the kitchen table, eating out of the casserole dish together. Each bite was bigger and more perfect than the last.

"Guess your grandmother was wrong," Mae said, her mouth full.

"About what?"

Mae swallowed. "She said there's no graduation day in the school of woods." She scraped the edges of the dish with her spoon. "I think we graduated, little sister."

Erin liked being called that. "If I ever get lost again in the mountains I hope you're with me."

Mae smiled, but underneath she looked as if she might cry.

Erin filled the casserole dish with sudsy water in the sink. When she turned around she saw Mae hunched over the table, asleep with the fork in her hand.

Quietly, she picked up the envelope and pushed through the back door. Slipping on her work boots, she walked around the side of the house.

Erin looked for a place to plant Lannie's letter.

No, not *plant* it.

Not now.

Bury it.

The oak tree stood at the edge of the driveway, just as it had eleven months ago. Erin dug a shallow grave with her hands, set the letter and envelope inside, and covered them with dirt. She brushed off her hands, wondering if she should say something.

Then she thought about the ranger's John Muir book and pencil stub. After finding them in the large pack, she climbed the oak tree to her special limb. She could barely make out the squiggles in the bark. Her initials, E. R. The tree had spent the past year healing itself.

She opened the book and flipped through the pages until she found her notes.

Questions
　　Without answers

A breeze picked up as the sky began to lighten. Rustling leaves made dancing shadows on the bark. Erin chewed the pencil, her bare feet dangling. She crossed out the first two lines and started over. She knew exactly how she felt, exactly what she wanted to say. But the words had to be just right.

Slowly she wrote,

Dear Mom,
　　This is your song...

AUTHOR'S NOTE

On July 29, 1996, I joined a group of backpackers on a five-day hike to Mt. Whitney (14,191 feet), the highest mountain in the contiguous forty-eight United States.

The rugged, glacially carved peak is located in the Sierra Nevada Range of Central California, on the east side of the Great Western Divide, a chain of mountains that cuts between the watersheds of the Kaweah River to the west and the Kern River to the east.

With a forty-pound pack on my back, I followed the rocky trail that zigzags from Horseshoe Meadows Campgrounds (10,000 feet) up the nearly vertical switchback to a boulder-strewn ridge called Cottonwood Pass. That's when it hit: a deadly summer electrical storm.

Two days later the headline on the front page of an area newspaper, *The Inyo Register,* read: "Hikers Survive Storm Strike: Lightning bolt kills horse, mule, as backpackers get struck unconscious."

Here's what the newspaper didn't report: My longtime friend Christine Peterson and I were on the ridge during the lightning strike. We witnessed the horror of the horse and mule dying on the trail. Three women in our party were injured by direct or indirect lightning strikes.

Christine and I dropped our packs and scrambled down the steep trail we had just hiked up to get help. Ducking at every blinding flash, we ran as fast as we could through gushing reddish mud. We were frantic, not knowing the fate of the injured women or the cowboy who was trapped beneath the dead horse.

Near the bottom of the switchback, the same cowboy ran by in boots, his yellow rain slicker flapping. "Where's my dog?" the cowboy cried, still in shock. "Have you seen my dog?" We subsequently learned that a group of hikers had dragged the dead horse off him.

An hour later Christine and I limped out of a pack station, crestfallen when we'd learned they didn't have a phone. Fortunately, we spotted a man in the parking lot, explained the situation, and hopped in his car. We drove down the mountain road until his cell phone snagged a signal. We reported the incident to the local sheriff's office, who dispatched members of the search-and-rescue team.

Afterward, Christine and I slumped at a picnic table in Horseshoe Meadows, shivering from the frightful experience, still in our drenched clothes. We heard the *thwack-thwack-thwack* of a U.S. Forest Service helicopter. We later found out that the three women were airlifted off the mountain to a nearby hospital, examined, and released. I don't know if the cowboy ever found his dog.

Months later, I began asking myself "what if" questions about that day. *What if* there had been a couple of kids on Cottonwood Pass during the storm? *What if* they had panicked and run the wrong way, cutting themselves off from their group? *What if* they had become hopelessly lost in the rugged Sierra Nevada with little food and few supplies?

Since the setting is real, I researched plant and animal life and geology in the southern section of the Sierra Nevada. I talked with people knowledgeable about the mountainous terrain. During a telephone conversation with a U.S. Forestry official I learned that even rangers sometimes get lost in the 900-mile maze of backcountry trails in Sequoia National Park. That nugget of information inspired me to include a lost ranger in my story.

My research included reading books by John Muir (1838–1914), a Scottish-born explorer, naturalist, and writer, who tramped through wild regions of the Sierra Nevada in the mid-1800s. His 1872 account of scaling a sheer boulder reminded me of Erin's rock climbing experience: "After gaining a point about halfway to the top, I was suddenly brought to a dead stop, with arms outspread, clinging close to the face of the rock, unable to move hand or foot either up or down. My doom appeared fixed. I must fall." But with a burst of energy Muir continued his climb: "I found a way without effort, and soon stood upon the top most crag in the blessed light."

All of us who appreciate the wilderness owe thanks to Muir, whose efforts to protect land, water, and forests convinced Congress to pass the Yosemite National Park Bill in 1890. This bill established both Yosemite and Sequoia National Parks.

In the summer of 2004, I returned to the eastern side of the Sierra Nevada Mountains to hike to Mt. Whitney. Instead of backpacking and camping, however, our group chose the one-day, 22-mile round-trip route. We left Whitney Portal Trailhead at 4 A.M. with the glow of our headlamps lighting the way. We returned seventeen hours later utterly exhausted. But we'd made it!

While on top of the peak, I celebrated with a picnic in honor of Erin and Mae: squashed peanut butter sandwich, hard cheese, leathery dehydrated fruit, and iodine tablets for my water bottle.

—S. S.

ABOUT THE AUTHOR

Linwood Fielder

SHERRY SHAHAN has written many books for young readers, including FROZEN STIFF, an adventure story set in the Alaskan wilderness. Just like her characters in DEATH MOUNTAIN, she got caught on an exposed ridge in the Sierra Nevada Mountains in a deadly electrical storm.

As a travel journalist, Ms. Shahan has hiked a leech-infested rainforest in Australia, ridden horseback in Africa's Maasailand, and been jostled in a dogsled for the first part of the famed 1,049-mile Iditarod Trail Sled Dog Race in Alaska. A longtime dance student, she has traveled around the world to study salsa and cha-cha-cha.

When not on an exciting adventure, Ms. Shahan relaxes on the beach near her home on California's central coast, pigging out on her favorite ice cream: Cookies n' Cream.